C-A-T Spells
Murder

C-A-T Spells Murder

Edited by
Alex Da Corte and
Sam McKinniss

KARMA

Cover by
Bill Schmidt

24 fiendish stories
and essays by

Dan Allegretto
Al Bedell
Alissa Bennett
Ian Bosak
Tommy Brewer
Charlie Fox
Noel Freibert
Francesca Gavin
Riley Hanson
Jonas Kyle
Sam McKinniss
Bob Nickas
George Pendle
Kaitlin Phillips
Tommy Pico
Sarah Nicole Prickett
William Pym
David Rimanelli
Collier Schorr
MT Shelves
Jeremy Sigler
Zach Smith
Amy Rose Spiegel
Jia Tolentino

Open Window

There's a shutter at the door
and your cat's your best friend
but everything is fine because you just know that
but did you leave the window upstairs open?
Was it supposed to rain tonight?
I can't remember
It's just the wind
I live in an old house
Is that thing coming back to get me?
Whatever happened to my cat's eye?
Its poor little eye
No, there's definitely definitely something upstairs
Is my sister home early?
Or is it the ghost of my sister?
Is that chain?
A chain saw?
What will I do with Dylan?
What will I do with my cat?
Are they here to take his other eye?
What about my eye?
Are they here to take my eye?

All I can think about is that scene where
    they cut up that guy's eye in that movie
You know the one?
Actual shaking
Actual screaming
He's coming for me
There's no way out of this room
This is it
he's coming for me
he's coming for me
he's coming for me
he's coming for me
I see him, I see him now
this is the last thing you are going to see alive
scream!
scream!
scream!
scream!

Contents

Charlie Fox

Scaredy Cat

Noise of flames, wolves howling, and a loop of shredding heavy metal guitar. Hell is a blood-red room lit with hot neon and swirling with fog banks of dry ice. SCAREDY CAT (Annie Clark) slinks in, dressed in a big fur coat and shades, eating a glittering cotton candy. She's only seen in silhouette, like one of the musicians in Fantasia *(1941), and shot with no extraneous material in the frame, like somebody in a portrait or confessional booth. She sits in a chair in a corner shrouded by the fog. She kills all the noise with a wave of a clawed hand, ditches the cotton candy, and lights a cigarette. Two huge wolves prowl around her.*

SCAREDY CAT: Being in Hell is so much fun. I always tell the creeps who hound me, "Dude, it's a never-ending party." I hang out all night with the disco ghosts, the fiery dogs, and the dead children with their black wings. I sing "Sweet Dreams" for the punk little devils and they go ape. Joy-gasm. I love that sound, like the circus is on fire.

A sudden burst of demented circus music. She emits an eerie purring noise.

Iggy Pop was here but he ran away. Sometimes I wake up in the snow as a thing without a brain, like a scare-crow or thunder or a cloud of weed smoke ... (*She fires up a fluorescent puke-green bong, takes a big hit and exhales lurid smoke like a nuclear power station.*) It's fun to not have any bones. And sometimes I fuck a hot fawn and we drift out to the jungle in this stolen convertible that reeks of cooked flesh. We melt. I lick up her blood like chocolate syrup. I blast "Purple Rain" and shiver like a scaredy cat. Desire is a weird beast—rip it open, slurp it up.

Two wolves howl the outro melody to "Purple Rain" by Prince. She kisses each one on the muzzle.

Thanks, boys. One of the Flying Monkeys who stays here, he's got the virus. He was into Triple X porn and opiates. He got it from boning the Bride of Frankenstein in *Horror Show IX* or from sharing filthy needles with nowheresville truckers, I can't remember which. I miss acid freaks. He told me the Wicked Witch sold all his brothers to labs for medical testing and they got sick. Now they're buried at this cemetery in New Jersey. He kept mumbling to me, "Say goodbye to my boyfriend Xanax, goodbye to my boyfriend angel dust, goodbye to my boyfriend OxyContin ..." He pumps the volume on the TV really high so we're in this horror movie. He was knocking back antidepressants and calling them "my candy." I just wanted to smash my head into the TV to stop the noise. He said, "I used to fuck like Godzilla, girl, I really did." And then he was just wailing like an orphan. I guess it's the fever. (*She plucks a ball of cotton candy from the cloud and playfully bats it into the dry ice.*) His mullet's kinda repulsive now but I guess it was hot once upon a time. Coke messed with everybody's radar so they fell in love with total garbage.

Two wolves pant and bark.

(*Dreamily singing*) "Somewhere over the rainbow / I'm gonna die ..." (*Normal voice*) Let me spike my 7UP.

She swirls a fluorescent green cocktail in a glass, splits a tranquillizer on its rim and slips in the sparkling powder. She stirs the cocktail with a black straw and slurps it up.

So the popular follow-up question to "What's it like in

Hell?" is, oh, "Was it weird when you first got there?" Yeah, indeed. They had me in that, like, video game. I wake up, green fluid oozing out of me into the bed. And I knew I was inside my childhood home but somehow it was not my house: everything was wrong ...

The silhouette of a devil playing saxophone sneaks in behind SCAREDY CAT and begins playing creepy jazz mixed with the noise of a lonesome breeze.

Outside my window, the sky was all Halloween orange and sizzurp purple. My old cat, Minx, was dead and stuffed. And I go downstairs and I'm there but ... it's not me. The other girl, she's this eighties cheerleader vixen with feathered hair, but she's got my face. She's gone Code Red, barking, "This is a planet of trash! A planet of trash!" and she sees me on the stairs and ... this evil scream just comes out of her like hot smoke. She thinks I'm a ghost. And I'm craving a beautiful dark wolf to leap through the window and rip her throat out but suddenly—

The creepy jazz turns demented; SCAREDY CAT headbangs.

— The devil's in the house!—

A shadow moves through the smoke.

— His seven black dogs on the leash—

Noise of huge wolves barking in a kennel, heavy on echo, to the demented jazz.

— Beautiful flames dancing all over him, and he just slays the other girl. I puked a kaleidoscope—gummy bears, roadkill, psychoactive mushrooms—

The sax solo writhes like a crazed snake.

— And it was magic.

The sax solo fades into something romantic but sinister, like goosebumps creeping over lovesick flesh.

— The hazmat balloon of her flesh is lying on the rug, all wet and leaking slop. The Devil comes close, purring in my ear, "Don't be frightened." I was always scared when I was a little kid. Anxiety was a vampire feeding on me. My sisters said I was a Martian.

And now I'm not frightened at all.

But I still can't sleep. I make a lot of phone calls. I call up my relatives in the dead of night and whisper to them: "Boo ..."

I tell them I'm an angel.

Or I tell my dad I'm rotting.

She lifts her arm like a swan's wing: it's covered in mysterious ooze. She lets it fall.

"Come over now," I say, "and watch me go up in flames."

She says something in the backwards language of the dwarf from Twin Peaks. *The lone guitar from "Sweet Dreams (Are Made of This)" by Marilyn Manson kicks in and, as the dry ice swirls, she sings the chorus with the enchanting vibe of a Disney witch.*

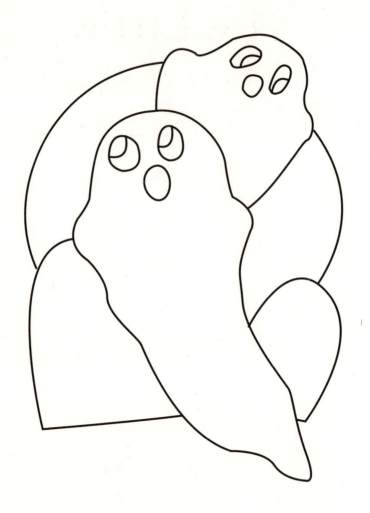

George Pendle

The Little Green Ghost

It was 1951 and I was being held in the camp at Changsong when I first saw the ghost. It was a short ghost, not much bigger than a child, and it walked through the bars of my cell like they were made of toothpaste. I'd had my left eyeball gouged out with a can opener the day before, so I could only see out of one eye. But I saw that little ghost come right up to me and, with its head tipped to one side, stare at me for a good long while.

Like I said, it was about the size of a child but it was not a child. Its whole face looked wrinkled and old. Its eyes were black but it glowed green from head to toe. And it had a big green nose too, like a gnome's, with a wart on it. I can't remember what it was wearing but it definitely had clothes on. Anyway it looked at me and I looked at it, and then it did something really surprising. It grasped its nose in its right hand and pulled it off. Pulled it right off. There was no blood, or ectoplasm, or anything like that. It just took its nose off and then, with a sudden lunge in my direction, stuck it to my face.

I was so shocked I didn't know what to do. There was no mirror in the cell, but I could see, glowing right in front of my one living eye, the ghost's warty nose on my face. I must have looked ridiculous because the little ghost stepped back from me and started laughing and grabbing his sides. His laughter was silent, you understand, but he was definitely laughing. Well, as he was laughing, Lim, one of my torturers, slammed open the door and my little green ghost disappeared in a wisp of green smoke. But he'd made a mistake. He'd forgotten his nose was still stuck to my face.

I tried to turn my head to the wall to hide it from Lim, who I figured would not be happy to see it, but he grabbed me by the hair and twisted my neck so sharply I was spun around like a top. It was then that he saw the nose and let out a grunt. He tried to grab it from off of my face but his hand just went straight through it. He looked at me angrily as if I was playing a trick on him, but I shook my head and hands and pleaded it wasn't my fault. So Lim wound up his right arm and punched me. His hand went straight through the green nose and hit my real nose with a crunch. Blood gushed out of it and I felt another tooth go. But when my eye cleared of tears I could still see the green nose glowing on my face and so, unfortunately, could Lim.

Well, he had quite a go at me that morning, did Lim. He used the hot bamboo spear and then the car battery. I screamed and screamed but the green nose stayed stuck to my face throughout. After a while he called in one of the other torturers and both of them looked at me and my green nose and scratched their heads as if they were looking at a broken-down car they didn't know how to fix. Well, they eventually left me and I pulled myself onto my concrete bed and curled up in a ball and dabbed at my wounds with my filthy clothes.

I was feeling pretty sorry for myself when what should happen but that little green ghost came waltzing back in. He stopped at the bars and, seeing me hunched over in an even worse state than before, began laughing again, rolling around on the floor laughing. When he got up he wiped his little black eyes and it was only then that he noticed he didn't have his nose. His fingers darted all over his face trying to find it, and then he looked up at me and saw it, and hurried over with a worried expression. But I certainly wasn't going to give him his nose back after he had laughed at me like that, so I stood up tall on the bed, and the little green ghost started jumping around beneath me, arms in the air, trying to grab his nose back. Every time he clambered up onto the bed I'd jump down, and when he got down again I'd clamber up. He was a poor excuse for a ghost, seeing that he could walk through walls but couldn't float. After a while he just sat on the floor cross-legged and began to cry little green tears. I didn't feel sorry for him one bit.

Well, all the noise of me jumping up and down brought Lim back to the cell. He was angry but I pointed to the little green ghost without a nose sitting crying on the floor and then at the green nose stuck to my face and he immediately understood. I don't know how he did it but he grabbed the ghost by its hair and dragged him out of the cell. There were some loud thuds outside and what sounded like a scream and then the green nose on my face slowly disappeared. Where it went or what Lim did to the little green ghost I was never entirely sure, but I do know one thing for certain: ghosts can be real dicks.

Alissa Bennett

Townsend Massachusetts (1987)

Our house was definitely sad after my mom died but I never thought there was anything scary about it until things started to go really dark. I guess that's the thing about evil. You're already through the door of the gingerbread house and shoving gumdrops in your mouth before you realize that the old lady inside is a witch; it isn't until you hear the car doors lock that you understand that the man at the wheel is going to fuck you up in ways you'll never recover from. All I'm saying is that sometimes you have to get up close to see what's going on, and by the time you figure out what's about to happen, it's basically way too late.

Were my sister and I depressed that summer? Of course. We were lonely and sullen, we were motherless, and if you don't know what that's like, well then good for you. Our dad was practically nonexistent—we saw him for an hour every afternoon before he left for his shift and heard him sneak back in late at night, trying to be quiet so he didn't wake us up, never realizing that none of us could sleep anymore anyway. He would open a beer and sigh and sit in his recliner and sometimes he would cry, but he never, ever asked either of us if we were OK. It didn't matter; none of us had anything to say to one another. I guess I am telling you all of this so that you can at least try to understand why it was so exciting when the phone calls started coming; in a way, the phone calls saved my life.

I don't remember the day that it started. Was it a Monday? A Wednesday? Who knows; every day of that summer had been exactly the same until that point, sitting in the TV room with the shades drawn and the fan on, *Sale of the Century* or *Days of Our Lives* flashing in the dark. Sometimes we would douse our heads with Sun-In and hang out in the backyard, hoping that something might happen to at least make us beautiful if we couldn't be happy. You can probably imagine what it was like when our phone started ringing; you were fourteen once, weren't you?

He sounded older, he sounded like a college boy when

he asked "Is Katy there?" and even though I guess I should have known better, I didn't care. It didn't matter to me. He told me that someone at school had given him my number, he told me that he wondered how we were doing, if we were OK. He told me his name was Jordan and that he was on the football team at Ridgeway High, lucky number seven. He told me that he would call me the next day just to check in, to make sure I was doing alright. Did we get to know each other over the next three weeks? I thought so, and it didn't feel so strange when he asked if he could take me out on a Thursday afternoon. I'd never been on a date with a boy before, and mostly I just figured this was how it went. It felt exciting to imagine meeting this stranger who was older and more popular than I was. The closer we got to the date, the more confident I felt that, even though life was mostly disappointing, sometimes it could also be fine.

I dressed carefully when the day finally came. My sister even said I looked pretty, and when the doorbell rang, I looked at myself in the mirror and felt pleased despite the uneasiness, the nervous drop in my stomach. "Katy!" Marie yelled from the foyer. "JORDAN'S HERE!" I felt like I was drifting away from myself as I walked down the stairs, I imagined every boring familiar thing falling away, and I felt like my whole life was going to open up when I opened the front door. I was right, but I was wrong too.

Jordan was small and strange looking, his brow was heavy and his clothes too large, I smelled the oil on his skin and in his hair despite the several inches between us, and the best I could do was murmur a depressive "Hi" at him. We walked to town together and even though I wanted to tell him that he was a scrawny liar and a fraud, I focused on just getting through it in a way that wouldn't make me look like the baby I truly was inside. Eventually, my ice cream cone started to melt. I didn't have the stomach for this Jordan person or his fibs or his dull conversation, I didn't feel like being nice to this boy who was a stranger in every possible way.

"Thanks for the ice cream," I told him when I dropped the rest of the cone into a garbage can right in front of his face. "I have to go home now," and I made a move to leave before he could try something awful like kissing me or asking when we would see each other again. I almost didn't turn around when he called after me to wait, but I guess I was curious, I guess I just couldn't leave well enough alone. "Does your mom ever come around?" he asked me. "Like, does your mom haunt your house with, like, her face hanging off?" I turned around and ran the whole way home.

—

Things seemed to go back to normal, whatever that means. Marie and I tried to start a diet and fitness plan, we did aerobics in the living room every afternoon at one, thinking that when we finally went back to school, maybe we would be attractive enough for normal boys to ask for our numbers and take us on dates that didn't end in disaster or humiliation. I told her what Jordan had asked and we started burning an old yellow candle sometimes to see if we could come up with anything, just to see if there was anything left behind of our mother, a person who felt as though she'd evaporated from planet earth. Did I feel anything when we held hands around the flame and asked her to please give us a sign? Not at first, but we kept at it, we thought that maybe Jordan had been some kind of messenger and that it was our duty to see the possibility through to some kind of conclusion. Sometimes the flame seemed to move when we asked a question. It was both comforting and scary to know that maybe our mother did see us, that maybe she saw every single bad thing we ever did.

One Friday night, I made popcorn on the stove and poured the unburnt kernels into a bowl for the two of us; we ate it while we watched a movie and thought it was just our nerves when the scratching started. "Did you hear that?" Marie asked me, and I lied and told her that no, I hadn't heard anything, that she was younger and much dumber than I was and she was only scared because of the movie. I didn't say anything to her when I went back into the kitchen and noticed that the leftover popcorn was gone. What was the use of both of us being scared?

There were signs, of course, and over the next couple of weeks we would wake up to notice that things that had belonged to my mother were moved or misplaced. Windows that we'd been careful to lock before bed would be agape by the time we woke up. Certain items of clothing would go missing and then turn up in strange places. I found a plastic Halloween pumpkin that had been in the basement on my bed. "Do you think it's her?" Marie asked me, and it seemed the only comforting explanation was to tell her yes, that our séances were finally working, that our mother was back. "I love you, Mommy," Marie started saying out loud every night. I felt ashamed for having disturbed something that I felt we ought not to have meddled with.

It's hard to pinpoint the second when I knew that there was something very wrong in our house, but if I had to try, I would say it was the night the television started flashing and we felt a banging underneath our feet. We ran to our room and cowered until it stopped and then stayed awake until our father came home to tell him what we had done, to confess the mistake we had made when we decided to tamper with the ghost of our dead mother.

I'm sure I don't have to tell you where this went, I'm sure you can imagine that our father thought us dramatic, dishonest even. "STOP THIS," he yelled when we had finished telling him that we had disturbed the spirit world and that our mother was looking for revenge. "HOW

DARE YOU," he screamed, and he didn't need to send us to our room because we understood immediately that there was nothing else to be done. We did our best to stay awake, Marie prayed, and I silently begged for forgiveness. "I love you, Mommy," I heard her say one last time before we finally fell asleep.

There is something about daylight that makes everything you were frightened of in the night seem babyish and stupid, and when we finally woke up I knew that it was my job to be the phony adult in the absence of a real one. "We have to go look," I told Marie, and even though she resisted at first, I eventually convinced her to go to the basement with me so that I could show her there was nothing wrong, that our imaginations had gotten the best of us for no reason at all. I took a flashlight and we crept down the stairs together. Are there words to describe what we felt when we saw what had been done while we were hiding in our bedroom? The words DID YOU MISS ME were spray-painted in red across the walls, boxes of Christmas ornaments strewn across the floor in broken heaps. We screamed and ran up the stairs and out of the house, we pounded on the first door we found and tried our best to explain what we'd found to nice Mr. Keller across the street.

"It's our mother," we told him. "It's the ghost of our mother." If he was skeptical, he didn't show it. Instead he walked us back to our house and asked us to show him what we'd found. I could tell he felt sorry for us; I felt that we deserved his pity whether we were crazy or not. I was somehow relieved, once we got inside, to hear the scratching again, this time from the door underneath the stairs. "What the hell is that?" Mr. Keller asked us, and we stood behind him and watched, somehow gratified that an adult was present to witness the moment our undead mother would murder us all. It seemed to take a very long time for him to cross the room and touch the doorknob. "Who's in there?" he said, and I could tell he was scared even though he was pretending to be brave for us. Did he expect someone to be inside? It's hard to say, maybe he thought it was an animal, maybe he thought we'd tricked him. When the door swung open and I heard his scream, I felt a flash of satisfaction run through my terror, I felt somehow glad to see the back of a person's body wearing my mother's best dress. I'm not sure if that will make any sense to you; I guess it's hard to imagine if you weren't there.

I don't remember Mr. Keller yelling at us to get out. I don't remember him swearing at us. I don't remember waiting on his lawn for the police to come or the moment when my father finally arrived. I only remember that it seemed like a year that we stood there staring at the house we lived in, understanding that we could never be there in the same way ever again. "I saw her," Marie cried. "I saw my mom. I saw her dress," and I held her hand even though I felt an incredible numbness very deep inside of myself. "Shhhh," I told her. "Shhhh, Marie."

—

The truth, I suppose, was worse than any teenage fantasy; the facts of the haunting were much more horrible than what we had constructed in our minds. It took me a minute to understand, when they finally brought him out, and despite the makeup and the dress and the bizarrely detached quality of his stare, I recognized right away that it was Jordan who had been living in our walls with us for those weeks in August, that it was Jordan who had rifled through our things and eaten our food, touched our clothes, and banged on our doors. "Did you miss me?" he asked as they loaded him into the back of the cop car, and I suddenly smelled the oil again in a way that I knew would be permanent.

I was afraid that, when we left the house, we would leave all our memories of our mother with it, that our childhood would be erased like a blackboard and that all we would have left were milky smears that no one could make any sense of ever again. I took the old yellow candle that Marie and I had thought conjured all of our bad luck and I keep it safe, just in case we ever decide that we need it again.

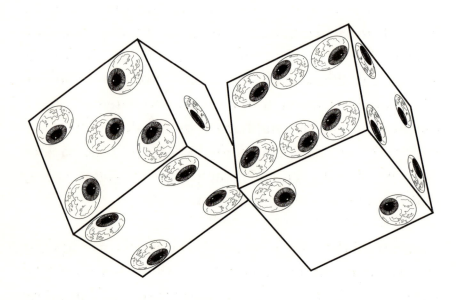

William Pym

The Car That Killed Us

1. It's time to rediscover America

In July 1991, in a cream-carpeted apartment in a complex for rich old people overlooking Boston Common, a television played a commercial imploring viewers to "Rediscover America." It was ninety-five degrees outside, heatwaves rippling in front of the expensive restaurants across the way. A modern air-conditioning unit, which whooshed, no rattle, used all its muscle to keep the temperature below seventy. The refrigerator looked after Tropicana orange juice, with pulp. The pebbled concrete terrace was out of bounds. It was too hot to walk 500 yards to get an iced coffee from Dunkin' Donuts. The baked-enamel sky called up the blue of Baghdad and Desert Storm, which had lit up our living rooms the past January on CNN, teleporting us to the Persian Gulf every night at primetime. We'd never seen that before. Versions of the "Rediscover America" spot came on every hour or so. The tagline, "It's time to rediscover America," was sung, and it flared out the airwaves on monotonous cable news commercial breaks. It was an expensively produced, perfectly finessed four-note jingle. It really carried through the silent apartment.

"It's time to rediscover America" was the core concept of Chrysler automobiles, 1991–92 advertising partnership with the media behemoth Time Warner. It was a panoramic campaign, including various versions of the slogan in print media ("Rediscover American Value" for minivans in *People* or *Popular Science*); the TV spots; and experimental tie-in stunts like "America's Favorite Music," a Warner-produced compilation tape of old-chestnut pop songs with American cities in their titles, placed in the glovebox of your new 1992 Chrysler Imperial. "Rediscover" was packaged and branded around the 500th anniversary of Columbus's run-in with North America. It was a big-agency, big-business campaign built monolithically around a single word. Now, to be clear, no one talks about this in 2018. It isn't taught in advertising school, as far as I know. Its makers' names aren't memorialized, or even recorded.

It wasn't a big deal by any means. It was one of dozens of dumb slogans selling stuff all day and all night over a long summer of having the TV on. And, most importantly, "Rediscover America" didn't sell any cars: Chrysler pulled Time Warner off the job and killed the campaign in the fall of 1992, before they'd even let their two-year contract run.

In the summer of 1991, however, if you heard that chorus of ladies sing the jingle at the right moment, with the sun turning windows to mirrors and the living room flooded white, hypnotized by the set, with the sound of bombs dropping on buildings still in your ears from the last chunk of rolling news, you could picture what "Rediscover America" was trying to sell. The car embodied adventure. America was tactile and health-giving and yours for the taking. The car was a conduit, a machine to help you reconnect, to take you away from the television and the city and modern life. Get out there, rediscover it, in a Chrysler car. You could readily picture returning soldiers from the war you saw on that TV, young, rattled guys, sitting there, just like you, being told to get up and go. For a moment, the ad connects. Buying a car is a good thing that keeps you connected to another good thing: America. Cars are machines of harmony and prosperity, taking you to a place of harmony and prosperity. And America is your place. That was the idea at its best, anyway. Like I say, no one remembers this campaign.

2. Art and Science

Whether they're aware of it or not, everyone remembers "Art and Science," the 2000s-era overhaul that rescued the reputation of Cadillac, the second-oldest car marque in the world. Cadillac was a knackered American name in the 1990s, not glamorous or innovative, producing rides for old people on old Chevrolet platforms. Otherwise-basic Chevys dressed for dinner were, obviously, not cool. The hook of the holistic "Art and Science" campaign was that design and technology could meet and collaborate, creating a new image of luxury and futurism. The "Art and Science"–era Cadillac Escalade was a chiseled, faceted, sculptural form over a huge SUV frame. No car had looked like this before. It had wide, paddled sides like cheekbones, meeting points like cut stone, and creases like folded paper. "Metal origami," ventured the *Fortune* magazine reporters at the "Art and Science" press day, where the 2001 Escalade was unveiled on the green of an eighteenth hole way up the Northern California coast.

It was an entirely new design language, and it hit immediately. The rendering and machining of these Cadillacs could only be done with the newest technology, and these technologies were speculative and searching, on the cutting edge. As a result, the energy of the "Art and Science" Cadillac was that of the future. Brave, dangerous, sexy. Everyone loved these cars. Escalades were fetishized as closely as female physiques in rap videos of the period, the camera lingering over the improbability of headlamp housings with a focus previously reserved for breasts and butts. In rap video's bling era, the top-spec Escalade or Escalade EXT—an outrageous hybrid of a five-seater SUV and a pickup truck—was a go-to for conferring luxury status. It could hold its own against diamonds. "Art and Science" design looked expensive because it *was* expensive; 3D-modeling and laser-cutting were expensive technologies. The car cost 74,000 dollars. But it felt right. "Art and Science" was the experience of riding capitalism and technology at one hundred miles an hour, barreling into the future together. While "Rediscover America" Chrysler of the early nineties promised to help us back, Cadillac of the 2000s led us to where we were going.

We are now in the 30th Street neighborhood of Philadelphia in the early 2000s, as "Art and Science" has begun to seep out. 30th Street Station, a large regional railroad hub, is an architectural object lesson of American Neoclassical purpose, with a radiant polychrome great hall and a dramatic porte-cochere overhang supported by fat, fluted columns: the city's number-one place to make out, say goodbye, or wait and think while smoking. Immediately to the station's south is a grungy, dark-stone 1970s tower I knew as "the talking building," as its top floors were a scrolling electronic display that announced community messages in yellow dot-matrix lights. You could read the announcements, or the periodic displays of the time and temperature, from ten blocks away. It was the headquarters of PECO, the electric company; the sign would occasionally remind you of this. It's a weird neighborhood, 30th Street, where the Schuylkill slits Philadelphia and West Philadelphia. There was a lot of nothing there for much of the 2000s. There was a drowsy string of adult movie theaters and jerkbooths, intact from thirty years ago; there were office buildings populated by hundreds of men and women, paralegals and such, in affordable business attire, only by daylight; there was the ghost of the Hoagie City that the model Gia grew up above in the seventies. The mega Trader Joe's supermarket on a derelict lot was still a few years away. There was 30th Street Station and there was the talking building. That's it. Which is why it's so surprising that no one said anything when, in 2004, a giant crystal began slowly forming over the train tracks.

The crystal grew to twenty-nine stories by the spring of 2005. It dwarfed 30th Street Station, turning the seventy-year-old structure ancient and stout, just like that. Irregular shards of glass curtain wall as tall as the building met at a sharp point, piercing the firmament. Depending on the position of the sun, the crystal either dissolved into the sky or beamed white light at you with apparent personal malice, enough to melt your dash. The crystal took on a name, the papers told us: Cira Centre. No one knew what or who Cira was, or why the word *center* was spelled European-style. Still no one knows. But we did know where it came from. The crystal was built with the same software and machines that built the "Art and Science" Cadillac: complex algorithms ensured the structural function and performance of the design, and sophisticated lasers carved the forms. It is a wonder. And the crystal carried the same promise as the Cadillac: this is what we have to take us where we're going, and we don't know where we're going, but it looks so good, so we shouldn't be scared.

3. The Spindle Grille

Driving on long arteries around eastern Long Island farmland in a Land Rover last summer, I saw no cars that truly surprised me. Backroad car culture in wealthy American enclaves like the Hamptons is a metronomic series of encounters: boat-size luxury SUVs, foreigns, basic rentals, pickup trucks driven by landscapers, and cherry restorations—a cream seventies Ford Bronco serving beach buggy with its jumbo tires, say—that make you whistle out loud. It's always the same. Last summer, however, as I lay in bed listening to the whip of a ceiling fan, a car popped into my head. The most grotesque face I had ever seen. Had I dreamed it?

I saw it again the next day, then, suddenly, everywhere. It was no dream. It was the Lexus spindle grille, a nose like no other. Variations of this grille had been rolled

out on 2014 models and had become, by 2017, something of a signature across the Lexus fleet. Once I'd seen
it, I saw it everywhere. The spindle grille has a curious,
unusual geometry. It looks like someone slipped in the
factory, or that part of it is broken. It is bottom-heavy
and drags; it looks uncomfortable. It doesn't seem right.
And it is anthropomorphically curious too. It looks, var-
iously, like a basking shark, an alien (the Predator from
the movie *Predator*, typically), or a bulldog. Indeed, in
the spindle grille I saw the logo for Red Dog beer, an
image that appeared in my head for the first time in
almost twenty years. Red Dog was a cheap American
lager drunk at parties and in college dormitories in the
1990s. Teenagers were convinced, in those days, that
the jowly dog face on the label bore a secret image of
Batman eating a girl out. So, that's what I saw when I
saw the spindle grille for the first time.

The new Lexus grille is shocking, it pushes you away. It
was designed this way to restore market share precisely
in this fashion, with drama and surprise, but it goes further than Cadillac's bracing "Art and Science" brand
refresh fifteen years before. It doesn't belong to us. It
isn't of us. It doesn't relate to anything we ever wanted
design to do for us. It doesn't reflect us or augment us.
It only dominates us, even though we, as its consumers,
were responsible for making it. Once you've seen the
spindle grille in many cities, on many kinds of Lexus,
you realize that it is here to stay. Before too long, you've

grown accustomed to it. Call it normalization. But this will never be anything other than an oppositional, sado-masochistic relationship. We will never be able to reconcile our desires—we will never be able to rediscover America or flaunt our faith in the future through a drivable diamond—through such a relationship. The Lexus with the spindle grille wants to do its own thing. And this is, thus, where our story will end. I have taken this sentimental journey, I have climbed this mountain of memories with you, in order to propose that we are losing control of the objects that we build in order to give our dreams form. We started this journey together, and now we have been left behind.

4. Millennials

None of this has anything to do with me. I am already too old to make a difference. Everything has changed. The future finally came, and we started living in it for real ten years ago, and there was no turning back. Technological dehumanization is a done deal. It's fine. It's just a new age. People want to live on phones now. The telephone is where they're going to look for their harmony and prosperity. Phones are where they want to find their reality. The real world is not for them, because the real world forces people to physically interact with each other, argue, be imperfect. Technological space is a space of fantasy and perfection, where we needn't believe in struggle, needn't concern ourselves with it.

Pick up a phone, and casually shrug the burden of having a body. Technology allows us to live this way, and if we continue to worship it and let it guide our lives, robots are for sure going to take over. And I'm not too fussed about that either. I feel fine. I don't feel sick in this world. The next revolutionary car won't have a driver. You'll be fugged out across the back seat, looking at your phone, indifferent to where you're going so long as you get there. I'll still be here, working to remember what is in the background of life on earth, waiting for you to get out of the way so I can see it more clearly.

Jia Tolentino

The Long Trip

Diana didn't have much room to move. She pictured the container like an egg, which it resembled—almost ovoid, mostly smooth. She lay strapped in her snug nylon harness, imagining herself unbuckling, floating into the center like a yolk.

She had wanted to do this her whole life. She was just a few hours out. Through the window it had barely gotten bigger. It was still a white nickel in the awful velvet blackness, sexless and luminescent, its shadows saying that same thing in the back of Diana's head, an indecipherable whisper, though it was getting clearer now, she thought—that was the whole point. When she had dreamed about this, she hadn't imagined the harness. Underneath it she was help-less: sinew at the shoulders, jelly everywhere else. It was hard to think about the speed of everything. Thousands of miles per hour. But it was peaceful. She opened her eyes and looked at the imperceptibly embiggening moon.

It had started fifty years ago, another life ago, with a video of Laika in seventh-grade earth science. The dog had a pink tongue and a face shaped like a bicycle seat. Her brin-dled ears flopped at the tip, like flowers. She had one paw up on her steel apparatus. It seemed like a miracle that the video existed—the scientists loading Laika in her capsule, tongue out. She orbited nine times. All of the dogs in the Soviet space program were street mutts; Laika would have never known she was so special, until suddenly, she was dying. One of the Russian scientists, the video said, had wept over Laika, and said, "Please forgive us." But there was nothing to forgive them for, Diana thought, in the dark, in class, and again. At this height you were seraphim.

And to think Diana had gotten away with it. She wasn't actually sick, which was her angle when she approached the company, spinning this as a Make-a-Wish sort of thing. But Diana wasn't a charity case; she had also made that clear from the beginning. At seventeen, she'd received an enormous secret settlement when a politician's daugh-ter, synapses bristling with coke and heroin, drove into the side of her car. Most people would have spent that money, but not Diana, who had avoided the great webs of efflorescing obligation in which people loved to entangle themselves, and thought about what you could really do with money and freedom if you asked. Anyway, Diana had a forged letter from Mount Sinai Hospital and 1.5 million dollars, and the company had been nothing but kind. She'd had to sign a confidentiality agreement, but that was just fine with her. She didn't want to explain this to anyone. She didn't think she really *had* to. People would start looking for nonexistent medical records; they would go on television and call her a freak.

In the egg Diana couldn't keep track of what was happening inside her body: she was bleary, and then suddenly alert. She didn't want to sleep at all, though they told her she would—the journey took three days. She had slept, just then, maybe. The moon looked closer, gleaming, orange-sized. Bigger. She had the pill in her pocket. She would take it before the shuttle started to burn itself up—just when her watch would start beeping—she had pictured it, opening her mouth just as the moon became all she could see.

Diana jolted awake again, gagging and shivering. Shimmering, she told herself. It was bigger. She made herself think of takeoff, the rush, the blitz, the unfathomable noise of it—a memory she could have spent decades eating for every meal. Beforehand, no one had asked her forgiveness. They honored the nobility of what she was going to do.

She banged her head on the wall, awake again, and screamed at the sight, though she could hardly hear herself. It was closer, enormous, a ghost frozen in bone. She pissed herself. The diaper was beginning to smell. She started shrieking, laughing, tears running down her face, gleeful. The whorls on the surface were turning into all the things they were supposed to, rabbits and faces and alien cities, but she knew that the moon was nothing but itself, pure and impartial, as precious as a fetus and as powerful as a god. The whispers in the back of her neck got more urgent.

She jerked alive again, vibrating on the inside, sicker. She threw up. There was blood on her palms, slits from her nails. She hadn't thought about this part much, even though they had warned her. The moon was cruise-ship size. The egg was a barnacle. She closed her eyes and willed her brain to do what it was supposed to—run the story. Bright flashes of sunlight, a breeze rippling the yellow curtains with the roosters on them, nettles stinging her chubby ankles, her hand thrust up into the darkness at a party she'd stumbled into, the curl of a cat tail around her wrist, glass doors parting as she stepped into the building at work. But that was nothing. She'd known it would all disintegrate here. Her life had begun when she saw the company representative at a trade show. She'd made some conversation and then just brought it up, blurting it, allowing herself to seem desperate, and he had looked at her with something like wonder in his eyes. Compassion. And once they brought her in, respect. It was all nothing less than what she deserved.

And it was easy, in the end, just a couple of months. Of course, it's different for a one-way voyage, one of the lab coats had said (people in the room shifted around, but Diana laughed, giving them permission to join her). The capsule was built for two, but the wonderful thing about private space exploration is that there weren't laws about how many people you *had* to put in a capsule, about what sort of things would merit the use of this *technology*—you could meet people's needs, you could bring them these sorts of experiences. She would have water, they told her, but no food. She nodded, in the elegant conference room, itching for it, aching, ready for her eyes to fill up with pure icy light. Under her harness, she started weeping. It was so close. No one had ever been here. No one had ever been so brave and so pure.

In the hangar, in Arizona, perfectly clean, the floors gleaming, four men watched the simulation pod. The first one shuddered. The second wore a gleeful and terrible sort of awe. "I'm still concerned that she won't take the pill," the third one said.

"She'll take the pill," said the fourth one. "Right when she's supposed to."

The pod, like an egg, rocked furiously on its pedestal, transporting Diana through space.

Collier Schorr

Ghostbusters

I could for the sake of portance shift this timeline, but I am not. I don't have to. Yesterday I sat in a darkened room at MoMA full of older men, European families; everyone is a tourist in a museum. I watched Nan Goldin's *The Ballad of Sexual Dependency* for the third time. I am much different from the me who watched it the first time. Less different, but certainly more sexual than the second time I watched it. The third time, they say, is the charm. The timeline I am talking about involves Maggie Nelson's just-as-popular book *The Argonauts*, which, like Goldin's slideshow masterwork, drops a lot of names, herds a lot of people in the room, talks about one's and others' bodies. They are not the same. Photography will never be writing. And vice-versa. I've done both and I can tell they are very different. But the timeline is this: I saw the slideshow yesterday and I read Nelson this a.m. and suddenly a sentence about Nan Godin's *Ballad*. I was jarred. But not stunned. The entire reading of *The Argonauts* invites connections between who you know, who you admire, who you yourself could pick an argument with. How I too loved Jane Gallop and how I was mortified to read Nelson's description of Krauss's deracinating of Gallop after a presentation. I'm thinking—I never met Krauss but I was always scared of her. People have had trouble with Krauss. Kind of like people have had trouble with Madonna. The big cheese gets shot through with the most holes. But to the moment of pictures and descriptions. Two identical feelings in me surface in the face of the slideshow and the text.

Cut to the first viewing of the slideshow, introduced by Marvin Heiferman at the nightclub The Saint, on 2nd Ave in the East Village. It's the eighties. I work in the gallery I will soon exhibit my work in. I live a few blocks away. I sit in the audience, prepared from what I have heard before that Nan will be late. Nan is always late. I'm fine with that. I'm always late as well. Finally the show starts. It's mesmerizing. It's about a world eight years older than me and also a world I live in now. I know a few people in the pictures. They are different than me. They are more photogenic. More of a flare for blowing out their brains with drugs and alcohol and actual orgasms. This is before I am taking pictures, so I bring nothing but words to the experience, the philosophies I have read, many of which contradict documentary photography. People are just starting to talk about snapshot photography, which will somehow release the makers from the rut and foul guts of Walker Evans history. Because these pictures aren't beautiful in their compositions, because they aren't even well-done, right, real photos, they are able to exist in the new smart art world as a bit of a pulse to accompany the pedantic text works, and a bit of actual ecstasy to accompany Cindy Sherman's parody of being looked at. I'm not photogenic and I'm not a photographer, but I do live with a beautiful junkie who is pictured in this slideshow. The pictures of her are older. When she is in her junkie prime, when the heroin acted like the fountain-of-youth potion in *Death Becomes Her*. She was beautiful; it's a beautifully insistent picture.

OK, the second time. Matthew Marks Gallery. I am older; the junkie is somebody else's roommate. By now I know more of the people in the slideshow. I have been written about by Cookie Mueller. I have gone to Cookie Mueller's wake. I was in the room when that picture was taken. It's the first time I have seen a dead body. The biggest difference though is that by now I have been photographed by Nan Goldin. She was on the floor in front of me, we were at a party at someone's house and she lifted up her Leica, the barrel of the lens honing in on my face.

I have little faith. I do not believe I can be photographed. And yet. Maybe I can. Maybe bathed in the yellow light that comes with no flash and a slow shutter speed, I will look like Patrick Fox, who someone said I once looked like. I will never look like his girlfriend Teri Toye or my friend Siobhan Liddell, who has been mercilessly trod out in countless *Ballad*s. Maybe I am photogenic. So that when I watch *The Ballad* for the second time, I am no longer just a bystander. I could be in there. So I watch, waiting for the flicker of recognition that comes from seeing yourself and simultaneously wanting to be recognized and not wanting to be seen looking at oneself. I'm not there. Throughout all the Velvet Underground and Depeche Mode and Edith Piaf I'm not a category and I'm not a song. It's as I suspected. Not even Nan Goldin could take a picture of me.

Which brings me to yesterday. The slideshow may be updated from when I last saw it. I remember other photographs being in it; I don't remember it being so categorized. Like bathtub pictures, black-eye pictures, pussy, kids, boys who look so good. I tell my sister-in-law from Turkey. No one in those pictures is wearing anything they bought new. Everyone is wearing old clothes they found or stole or bought for $5, which is why everyone looks so good and wears a lot more color than people do now. I am waiting for my picture. It's a wonderful way to keep feeling anticipation even after I have seen most of these pictures and maybe I'm thinking the slideshow is a bit long. A bit too many pictures of Siobhan and Brian. But mainly I'm anxious my sister-in-law might be bored. For me, I see Cookie again, I see my Edwige behind the bar, I see the dead people obviously and I am still not there. I'm missing.

Which then brings me to this similar moment in Maggie Nelson's book when she quickly skips over Nan to get to a photograph by A.L. Steiner and then segues into a parenthesis mentioning a few other artists' names. And I'm not there. I didn't expect to be. I don't know Maggie Nelson, I'm not from L.A. And yet, we look for ourselves, don't we? Our egos demand it. And I wonder how much more excitation there is in being a ghost than being present. I have seen *Ghostbusters* twice, remarkably both times in movie theaters. The first time, that would have been my only option. This second time, seeing a remake, to really enjoy this postmodern experience one must return to the source. The dark womb of the theater. I'm sitting with my girlfriend and next to an actress and her children, her face almost unrecognizable because she has just had a baby. The baby is absent, the boys are with her. The movie starts to play and I start to worry if these kids are too young for this movie. There is a drawing of breasts and I worry they will be uncomfortable, even though their big, nursing, movie-star mom must surely breastfeed in front of them. Afterwards, I think about the photo of the Cologne women artists Charline von Heyl, Jutta Koether, Cosima von Bonin, and a few others I don't know. They are posing outdoors with guns in their hands. The photo is a re-creation, a remake of a similar photo of male artists holding guns. Or did I imagine that. Maybe it's male artists in their boxer shorts? In their wife beaters. I'll go back and check this in a moment, but let's say it's a remake and that after seeing *Ghostbusters* I'm very interested in the ways in which women remake things, usually made by men. Are they remakes, then? Are they not entirely new? Is that the particular adrenaline of those kind of projects, that we have never seen "that" image before, with our faces in it? Our hands, our hips. The recognizing of oneself as well as the missing us. I'm obsessed with what that photo of me looks like. At the time I thought, I'm not protected by nostalgia. It will look too now and therefore not a memory, not shrouded in the fanciful light of distance. I won't look young enough or special because I'm not yet special. So, when I watch *The Ballad* the third time I am ready for the younger me, ready for the Patrick Fox lookalike, the curly black hair. I'm hoping it's shorter so I look like the actor from Jim Jarmusch's *Permanent Vacation*. I want to be in the boys' section. I'm not there. Funny, I was just last week in Bob Dylan's bus at Shangri-La Studios. Photographing myself underneath a circular window, pantheonic light pouring down. Proving what?

Kaitlin Phillips

School Shooters

Not counting losers, I know five types of people in New York: grifters, geniuses, school shooters, rich people, and art dealers. Most of these people are alcoholics, and got very good at their jobs without having to resort to criminality, except in the most banal and unavoidable ways. I think there are a lot of people I know worth being scared of downtown. Who you're afraid of says something about who you are and what you do. If you're an artist you're supposed to be afraid of the rich people in your studio, and grifters at your openings. Personally, I'm afraid of my father, who isn't even in New York, but like all boomers, his rising sign is school shooter.

I'm not afraid of rich artists on principle.

Boomer Artist, my ex-fiancé, he told me about the best funeral he's ever been to, when the father of his French art dealer died. The entire party sailed out into the middle of the Mediterranean to scatter the ashes, but when the moment came, Pierre or Hugo, or whatever, couldn't get the container open, so he just turned and jumped into the sea, clutching the remains of his father. Apparently he bobbed there for a while, using the urn as a buoy. (Classic art dealer.)

It's a movie trope, so I guess it's boring, but I did not expect that I would get my stepfather's ashes blown back into my mouth during his ceremony. We weren't on a schooner on the Mediterranean, obviously, but crowded onto a pontoon boat on our lake in Montana. I'm still terrified I swallowed him. I have this dream where I'm throwing up a black bile compound of dad's ashes and scraps of plastic, clutching a pale-pink toilet bowl in a carpeted bathroom.

I'm not afraid of Boomer Artist, even though he is a European. I suppose he should be afraid of me. Afraid of my putting his text messages in print. ("I had a surreal wet dream about you tonight. My penis was telescopic and released.") This I received in the year our twenty-year-old Lorde sang: "I bet you rue the day you kissed a writer in the dark." (A genius.) In Boomer Artist's defense, he's better IRL. Like, his marriage proposal was funny: "I like real estate and women, I want to combine my interests, and make you my property." He's a Sagittarius, like my boyfriend, which is neither here nor there except to say that Sagittariuses are the most self-actualized, which is why they can date grifters (like me) without losing their sense of self.

I wouldn't say I'm afraid of it, but that hotel-style Mediterranean smorgasbord that comes with the egg in the dainty little silver cup ... Boomer Artist always ordered that. I still don't know how to crack the damn egg. Now I don't want to humanize him but, according to the Mitford Nazi, you know who had impeccable table manners? Hitler.

Because I thought I was getting married, I did make an effort to improve myself this year, and accepted an assignment from the *Times* magazine "about table manners" as a means to con myself into reading turn-of-the-century books on the topic. I only wrote down one thing in my notebook from my readings, about young Americans traveling abroad. "She should be particularly careful if she is young and pretty not to allow strange men to scrape an acquaintance with her."

Some background: The last time I was in Europe, when I moved to Scotland at twenty, I was terrified I wouldn't be able to find a Percocet connection analogous to the one I enjoyed across the Atlantic. All I had finagled from emailing everyone I knew for "friends abroad" was one invitation to a literary party in Edinburgh. I went to the party, where I was properly shunned for inquiring maniacally about painkillers by everyone but a boy who said he'd give me some in exchange for a blow job. (When we left the party, I ran right into a street pole, so he kindly let me take them on the street on credit.) We had sex on my desk; he showed me his stepbrother's knife. The bruise on my forehead really enhanced my visibility in town, turning purple, then green. Two weeks on, I still hadn't got him to leave my single-room occupancy. A person in my Brecht seminar said that he was "alarmed" to have heard rumors, and he thought I should know this, though he felt bad about being the one to tell me, that I was hiding a guy who had raped a young girl at knifepoint. Blah, blah, blah, mortal danger.

Of course I thought about being afraid, but I couldn't really get it up. It was true he had run his knife across my collarbone, and between my breasts or whatever, but that was long ago and he'd gotten bored with it. But the fact was I'd already been habituated to my houseboy (whom only now do I recognize as a classic school shooter masquerading as a grifter). The information that I was harboring a criminal only proved that I was having an authentic experience abroad (there are a lot of criminals living in Western Europe).

As a grifter myself, I have designed my life around allowing strange men to *scrape* an acquaintance with me: school shooters, rich people, art dealers, other grifters. I'm ONLY afraid of men who are mistaken for geniuses.

Of my conquests, only my first boyfriend (a backcountry plumber) and my boyfriend (an outsider artist) seem to me geniuses, and not only because their professions demand they know how to use their hands.

Not that I feel safe in New York!!! This man hit on me on the subway, and when I didn't respond, casually pulled out a manual entitled, "How to Represent Yourself in Court." And, my god, the city is full of my ex-boyfriends' ex-girlfriends. The DIY Gen X women. My boyfriend—his first ex-girlfriend, at my age, she was giving herself coffee enemas in the bathroom. Just squatting on the floor, holding coffee in her ass for hours. These dolls she made out of cardboard are all over our house, from when she left New York forever to focus on her autoimmune disorder. (Genius.) I won't speak here of my boyfriend's ex-girlfriend with late stage Lyme disease, other than to say that it was much more chic in the nineties when people pretended to have brain tumors. (She's a forty-year-old school shooter.)

I wouldn't say men are afraid of me. Even if my boyfriend says I'm the last millennial he'll ever date. I understand him. As an anarchist, he's sensitive to the tyranny my lack of independence represents. I don't think he's going to dump me though; there's a line in a Charles Simic poem about this: "PHONE SEX WITH PERSEPHONE IN HELL, the ad said."

Jeremy Sigler

Raskolnikov

Feel like I just gave it all. Never seen the bowl so full. I may jump on the scale. Just to see. If I made it down to 167.8. I've never felt so goddamn skinny.

And so deserving of rest. Like, I just came out of surgery. And am now in recovery. Like still hooked to the iv. But stable.

Minutes ago, I was like breathing loudly and limping down Hicks. Like I was about to have an epileptic seizure.

It's like I'm here on morphine now. Haven't moved a muscle in thirty minutes. Just feeling ... relief.

Think I'll have a little lunch. Fill back up. I'll check and see what's in the fridge. Bacon, mayonnaise, corn tortillas, shallots, hot sauce. Just had three tacos. Lettuce! BLT tacos. Absorbed the remaining grease in paper towel. Dishes in sink. Public radio on. Too loud. Turn it down. Turn it off. Before the name gets mentioned. I'll give you a hint. No fuck that. Think I'll type T into my screen and see what choices I'm given. Trump? Trump? or Trump? See what they want me to have on my mind. You guessed it. I won't say it.

And the top choice for A is ... Alex Ross *New Yorker*. Haha. So personal. Love it. I was looking him up the other day to see if he had ever written on Beethoven's 32 Variations in C minor. Gould plays them like the Goldberg Variations. It's really funny.

Anyway. Sort of way. Anyway ... I'm really having quite the industrious afternoon. What am I doing? I'm usually so lazy. But now I have this new work ethic. Now I delete. Deletion is what I do. Like for a living. It's my job. I delete junk mail. The second one comes in. It's paying off too. I feel great about it. The last email that came in from Uniqlo is no longer sitting there taking up space on my cloud. And you know I pay for that unlocked locker. Neither is the email from the Guitar

Center, reminding me that Telecasters are on sale, taking up space.

I got them off my cloud. Hey Hey You You get off of my cloud. I am singing that. I'm like a working man now. I don't just check my email all day. Passively. Lazily. Now I delete shit. I tidy up my inbox. Big time. I'm busy as shit! Kind of like a doctor on call. Or a janitor on call. I'm staying ahead of the game. No not really.

Raskolnikov wasn't on call. Or was he? He wasn't busy. Or was he busy steering clear of anything that could be remotely considered a responsibility. He was without responsibility. Responsibility-less. Less is more. That way he could feel God, I guess. Not a bad place to be, in God's headlock.

Or is God less an arm and more a gaze? Are we all under the gaze of God? You know he .... Um, a, maybe when referring to God, I should use the gender-neutral pronoun They. God now goes by They. OK?

They might say: "I'm disappointed in you for wasting the time I've granted you." They might say: "I'm pretty disappointed in you for, like, only doing two things all day." Or They might say: "Congratulations, you have finally realized that I have no requirements."

But of course Raskolnikov began to wonder if he was

someone else's responsibility. Like his mother's. Or even his sister's. Or his sister's boyfriend's. "Is it possible," he asked himself, "to be nobody's responsibility?"

And after he listened to the old drunkard in the tavern talking shit out his ass all afternoon, saying things that are translated into English as "I get drunk so I can feel God's disappointment in me ..." I forget. I have it written down. Somewhere. But should a poet write from notes? Isn't that cheating? It is cheating. It's gotta come right from the keys. Gould is God. Gould is They. I love the chair. Don't you? Did it ever collapse while he was playing? Probably.

So, Raskolnikov was back out on the street in a daze of irresponsibility when he encountered a rag-dollish prostitute in her teens who was herself a nubile drunkard. And somewhat bloated. And he thought: "Maybe it is my responsibility to protect her. Maybe I have to come out of early retirement. Get back in the game. Maybe I ought to somehow shield this stranger as if she were my own daughter?" You know?

It may have still been on his mind—what the drunkard in the tavern had been saying. I think his name is Marmalade. Anyway, he admits with total shame that he was once so penniless and hard up for a drink that he had the nerve to sneak into his daughter's bedroom and steel her stockings and pawn them. It's sad. But also moving. The way Raskolnikov, or maybe I should call him by his full name this time—Rodion Romanovich Raskolnikov—flags down this cop, announcing proudly, "Excuse me Mr. Officer. I'm a student. My name is Rodion Romanovich Raskolnikov." The same way Don Quixote might have announced, "I'm a noble knight errant from La Mancha. My name is Don Quixote."

Raskolnikov thinks he knows right from wrong at that moment. But then he has a second thought: "who knows what one knows." And, is it not a student's job to not know? To be a noble warrior of all the ideas?

This is when Rodion Romanovich Raskolnikov has this awful memory, triggered by the street he is walking down, of a recurring nightmare from his childhood. In the dream, he walks with his father past a tavern on the way to visit the grave of his younger brother, and he sees a man with a big horse-drawn wagon of sorts, but more like a flatbed. And the man is yelling for everyone to "get in," waving his hand in the air, offering this big group of drunk noisy rowdy sporty rich folks a ride. He's like your basic parked Uber driver, waiting for the concert to let out. And he then starts whipping the fuck out of his old feeble horse, trying to get its knobby old legs to move, trying to get it to somehow roll this impossibly overflowing load of assholes forward like one inch. And so the dream is stuck in the mud horror.

Then the student wanders on to the next chance moment. Where he encounters another cop. This one is playing billiards and chatting with a student. Is he hallucinating, he asks? Then Raskolnikov remarks how coincidental it is that they are talking about the exact thing he was thinking about at that exact moment. As if he is encountering himself in three-dee. As if he is having an out-of-body experience. He hears the student claim to hate the soft sweet pawnbroker. Who is in fact like a disease, as he sees it. A contaminant to the world. And he thinks she should pragmatically be exterminated. So that her money can then be sprinkled around and put to good use. Like killing an ugly old pharmacist, robbing their entire supply of asthma inhalers and handing 'em out on the street corner down in Baltimore's inner city. (I mean come on! The kids can't fucking breathe!) Anyway, he imagines, I guess, the prostitutes all being set free by his single act of eugenicide.

Then the friendly cop interjects, in a wonderfully authoritative tone: "Would you do it? Would you like to be the one to kill her?" And the student answers, "Hell no, of course not." He knows, after all, that he is just a student. Using his mind to, I guess, theorize … to stage mental kickboxing matches in the cage of his brain. It's not his place in life to actually dirty his hands with actions that speak louder than words, or acts that might even ignite his conscience, or a sense of paranoia.

But Raskolnikov, who is basically spying on himself, wants us to know what's on his mind. He wants us to hear him having sex through the wall.

That being said, what's really in my mind right now? Or on my mind. Surfing this dinky wave. What's really going on in here? I guess I would have to say, the first thing that comes to mind.

So here it goes: I said in class that Jesus was just another version of Moses. Just younger and skinnier. Maybe a little hotter. Sexier. I said this to a class full of women. Freshmen. And they smiled, liking the simple idea, I guess. I said: you know, if that's your thing? If he's your type? Maybe you're more into the Moses type? Then I explained that Nietzsche was all about this giant, like really oversized mustache. Like the biggest mustache I have ever seen. The biggest mustache in modernity. Which is when I shifted my weight to my other foot, took one hand off the lectern, grabbed at my own stubble, and confessed that I had, perhaps on some unconscious level, chosen not to shave, so that I would have the makings of a stash. Maybe it was because I knew we would be talking about Zarathustra. And the Antichrist himself. And, you know … I wanted to be able to sort of grip my face by the spongy wiry gray hairs and tug my lip ever so gently, urging the words to inch even closer to the edge. Urging my words to consider being spoken. Urging intuition, as well, to tug lightly at my brain.

Dan Allegretto

The Call Came from Inside the Pool

It was the summer of 2005 in a small town upstate called Elmira. For me it was the year between junior and senior year of high school and I ruled the world because after years of being moderately whack I was finally popular. I was best friends with all the cool girls and the boys had to like me or else I would squeal on them to the volleyball team. Season 2 of *The O.C.* just had its finale in May. I looked like Seth Cohen but in my mind was a total Marissa.

It was a super-hot day and I had nothing to do since I got straight A's my entire life, my parents never made me get a job in the summer. I think they actually just got divorced and my dad moved out but I don't know lol I repressed a lot during this era. Anyways, so I'm wading around in my above-ground pool that was fifteen feet in diameter and three feet deep. This meant that while standing up the water level was well below my belly button (I was very tall and skinny and sublimely beautiful). The pool sucked to be in because the bottom had all these divots my brother's friends would get stuck in and roll their ankles and complain to their parents about. I always had the cordless phone on the edge of the pool because it seemed chic and I didn't want to get my Virgin mobile flip phone wet.

So I'm just chilling out and I hear the loudest siren I've ever heard in my entire life. It's like when you imagine a nuclear fallout and a horn you've never heard before blasts throughout the entire town. "Well, this is fucking annoying as hell." It wouldn't let up. The cordless phone rings. It was my mom calling from work. She taught a GED program for adults who dropped out of high school to get their diploma. I thought that was noble. "Danny, where are you?" "By the pool, obviously." "You need to get inside and lock the doors." "Ew, why?" "Two inmates escaped!"

My parents' house was three houses down from a maximum security prison, which never seemed that strange to me, until now. Mad annoying. I had to get out of the pool. That explains the siren at least ... but what if they were lurking around the perimeter? How am I going to do this? I would peek over the edge very slowly and then quietly mince to the other side and peek over there. I did this for an absurdly long time. Enough is enough! I scrambled up the ladder, grabbed the cordless phone, and hightailed it inside. No time to grab the towel. Dripping water all over the linoleum floor, I didn't know what to do next. Should I log onto AOL or something?

I can't remember how I actually got this information but let's just say I turned on the TV and the local news was going absolutely buckwild. Two inmates, both serving life sentences without parole, had escaped. One brutally murdered his pregnant wife and the other shot a taxi driver in the back of the head with a shotgun for seemingly no reason. And now they were on the loose, probably right in my own backyard. And that godforsaken fucking siren was still howling.

I couldn't be Marissa Cooper next to the pool with all this racket or these damn criminals running around all over the place. More details developed in the newspaper the next day. The front page of the *Star Gazette* was one of the most bizarre things I had ever seen. It was a flash photograph of two papier-mâché heads with crudely drawn faces and long gray hair glued to the top to resemble an actual human. Well, they didn't. They looked like someone dipped Wilson the volleyball from that Tom Hanks movie in glue and rolled it around the floor of a barbershop. The inmates had stuffed their beds to simulate a sleeping body while they escaped through the roof and reattached the ceiling they had been chipping away at for months with toothpaste.

They pulled a Rapunzel, or any escape story for that matter, and rappelled from the roof with a series of bed sheets tied together. The first guy made it safely, but the second guy was not so lucky. He fell from over thirty feet and shattered his knee or broke a shin or some shit. I don't know, his leg was fucked the hell up. In a shocking twist, the noncrippled inmate stuck by his cellmate and didn't abandon him, unlike many disloyal people that I happen to know. This was the first day of the rest of their lives lol.

At Sunday dinner I talked to my uncle about this whole catastrophe since he was a corrections officer at the prison. He actually knew both of these men personally. He pulled out a painting that was the size of a poster that one of the inmates made. Two bald eagles bravely soared above a river valley with an American flag stretched between their beaks. Two F-14 fighter jets patriotically blasted above them. It was horrifically rendered in acrylic and this man clearly had severe mental probs. We all just want to be free, I suppose. Did the eagles symbolize the two inmates? Were they like ... gay with each other? Who knows!

I thought I was going to be murdered in my sleep or even worse, while awake wearing something Fugly. We lived in a really old house and breaking in would be a cinch. Six days went by and the only traces the authorities could find of these men were some hunting cabins they had broken into outside of town. They couldn't get very far because of the bum leg, mind you. My summer of feigning to be an Orange County skank wasn't really shaping up. I couldn't peacefully get drunk or high in the woods with my friends because ruthless murderers were on the loose. And forget about using my dilapidated above-ground pool.

Another full week went by (siren still popping off) and a breaking news alert came across the TV. We hadn't turned it off since the day of the fateful escape. Unimpressively, they had been caught behind Jubilee supermarket the next town over, seven miles away. Thank god, I guess. It was kind of thrilling and horny though to be honest. I wasn't having sex but the siren as a soundtrack to teenage lovemaking would have been cool.

Days later the inmates were interviewed about the details of their escape. The only part I remember is that after busting loose they walked through my backyard in the middle of the night ... right next to the pool. *My fucking pool!* Sometimes I would take little secret night dips, can you even imagine? "Go ahead, escape from prison. Let's have sex." I should have been screaming and throwing furniture into it all summer like Marissa, instead of fearing for my life.

A year went by and they finally put up a fence around the prison, which, by the way, happened to be right in the middle of town. Who would have thought? Maximum security prison. A fence. Brilliant. Perhaps a moat would have been more fitting.

I graduated high school and my mom sold the pool on Craigslist. Don't ask me how someone moves a fucking pool but it was gone. Marissa Cooper died at the end of Season 3, and so did a part of me. Season 4 was lame and then I went off to college and began my adulthood, which was eleven years ago and the whole time since has also been very, very, stupid.

David Rimanelli

Shelter

We were a select company at a summer dinner party given by an art dealer and her husband, a collector, at their house on the North Fork of Long Island. At one point, I overheard an interior decorator, and one not entirely without taste, talking about a house done up in what he called "Jacobean style." My interest was piqued, and I interposed that I did not think that this style, unlike Louis XVI or Federal, was one that could possibly be adapted to contemporary living. "Well then," the decorator continued, somewhat peeved by my remark, "how would you describe the Jacobean *look*?" Caught off guard, I mumbled something incoherent about Hatfield

House, rebuilt in 1607–11 by Robert Cecil, first Earl of Salisbury and Lord Treasurer to James I, then nattered on further on court portraiture as practiced by Larkin, Peake, and de Critz, before falling back on miscellaneous details of Cecil's political career. "The King's misuser, the Parliament's abuser, / Hath left his plotting … is now a rotting." But this satirical epigram inspired me, and I felt suddenly and aggressively revivified, as if possessed by the *daimon* of snotty superciliousness, I intoned: "For our purposes, it corresponds to the décor of Vincent Price movies. Pitilessly uncomfortable chairs upholstered in heavy, often tattered damasks, winding staircases that perilously lack balustrades, branching silver candelabras, portraits of desolating ancestors, armor, stained-glass windows, long dark corridors. Seventeenth-century dust and veils of cobwebs. Campy and creepy." The decorator conceded that his information must have been faulty, as the residence of which he had spoken was destined for publication in *World of Interiors*. "So Jacobean's not pretty, right?"

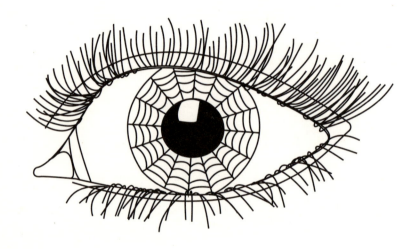

MT Shelves

Butt Dial

High school was stupid so far but at least I had a new phone. It was an old Android that used to be my Dad's. He suffocated while trying to blow up an air mattress. "I want you kids to take something to remember Dad," said Mom after the funeral. She said it over the intercom of the school bus. Driving it was her job, and in order to get all twenty of her sons to the funeral, she borrowed the bus. And painted it black.

My parents didn't want to kill anything, not even sperm. They were afraid of the dead coming back to life ... with good reason. My brother Conrad drowned in a hot tub a year ago. One night he came back to life. We were watching TV and Conrad came on the screen to demand his allowance in back pay. My Dad didn't know what to do. He had nineteen other kids and each of us only got a quarter every week. So we turned him off.

I always woke up earlier than everyone else. Our bedroom was like a hostel with rows of bunk beds. I looked in my cubbyhole—the phone was not there. As I bent over searching I felt my butt turn to ice. "Where's my quarter?" said Conrad. I turned. My phone was floating behind me with my brother's face on the screen. "Give my phone back, Conrad!" I shouted. "Oops, butt dial!" said Conrad. The ghost phone shot into my asshole with a sound like a straw sucking the last ounce of soda out of a cup.

I was late for my second day of school. "You're late," said Mr. Philbert. "I lost my phone," I said. "What does that have to do with anything?" said Mr. Philbert. "It's my alarm clock," I said. "And it has sentimental value." "Oh really?" said Mr. Philbert, becoming interested. Suddenly I realized that night had fallen and we were alone in the classroom. "What's happening?" I said. "I hypnotized you," said Mr. Philbert. "You've been standing there for eight hours. The school is closed and everybody has gone home. And now I am going to kill you. "What did I ever do against you?" I said. "Was it my persistent mouthing off?" "I'm in love with your mother," said Mr. Philbert. "I've loved her ever since she first started driving the school bus." "Wow," I said, surprised. I didn't think such a thing was even possible. Mom was hot once, but years of giving birth had made her body look like a turkey's. "And I'm going to kill all her children, one by one." said Mr. Philbert. "Why?" I said. "You're a financial burden," said Mr. Philbert. "That loser veterinary assistant that she was trapped with just kept knocking her up." "No one says that about my Dad, he was an honorable man," I said. "Pffft!" said Mr. Philbert. "He was a well-known animal fucker. People used to get their cats back from the vet with their assholes all stretched out." Whether this was true or not, it reminded me that the ghost of my brother was still crammed into my rectum. "How are you going to do it, Mr. Philbert? How are you going to kill me?" I said, stalling for time. Mr. Philbert had a smouldering beaker in his hand. "I'm going to pour this hydrochloric acid down your throat and it will burn your guts away." "My brothers are going to fucking kill you!" I screamed. "Already dead," laughed Mr. Philbert. "Your mother and I poisoned them last night. Didn't you notice that none of them woke up this morning?" "They were asleep. I always get up first," I said. "Normally," said Mr. Philbert. "But this morning, your alarm didn't go off, did it?" He moved closer to me, close enough that I could see his long eyelashes, the stupid smirk on his face, the pores on his pointy nose. My feet were rooted to the floor due to hypnosis.

Suddenly my brother called me from the inside of my rectum. It was a weird feeling, like when you use your car to talk on your phone, except I was the car. "Greg? This is Conrad." "What should I do here?" I said. All this conversation happened telepathically and in a split second. "Shit me out so I can get this bastard," said my brother. "He's the one who killed me when I was hot tubbing. He killed Dad too, by prefilling the air mattress with chlorine gas."

I squeezed my abdominal muscles. Nothing happened. "I can't do it, Conrad!" I gasped. "It's more about relaxing than about exerting yourself," said my brother encouragingly. "Look, if a cat can relax its asshole enough to take a human-sized prick, you can pass a little phone out your rectum." "How do you know so much about cat assholes?" I said. "Jeez, Greg," sighed Conrad. "Me and Dad used to double-team them when I was working as his assistant at the veterinary clinic." "God, is my whole family completely perverted?" I said. "Better you know now, Greg. Sometimes it takes a crisis to get the truth to come out," said my brother. "You're the only one of us left—the only remaining trace of Dad's kind and gentle nature. Shit me out, Greg." "Do you still want money, Conrad?" I said. "I don't care about that now, Greg," said my brother. "I just want the family back."

Suddenly I could do it. I relaxed. And that was all it took.

Al Bedell

Rolling Marbles Down a Hall

I suspect most people wish that nighttime could last longer. Magical things happen when the moon is out, wishes are made on stars and lullabies are sung to babies. Candles shine brighter in the dark. You are not required to work during the nighttime. It's a time designated for rest and rejuvenation. You can hold someone you love as you breathe together softly, or you can just sleep. You can turn your mind off for hours and forget about your problems, or you can dream and enter a world more ideal than this one. For most people, nighttime is peaceful but doesn't seem to last very long as they are forced to rise with the sun.

For others, like myself, the nighttime is frightening and relentless. For sufferers of insomnia, nighttime is a punishment to endure. Insomniacs fear darkness, the stillness, the deafening quiet, the painful longevity of a single minute. Minutes turn to hours while sleeplessness amplifies your darkest thoughts that you otherwise get to ignore during day-to-day distractions. The idleness of night grants you access to a world much less pleasant than this one—the depths of your own mind. Debilitated in bed, chained by thoughts that you cannot escape, spiraling into a well of your greatest anxieties. Nighttime is the loneliest time. You count to two million and literally pray to god for just an hour of sleep. You consider calling your parents to apologize for everything you've ever done wrong. Sometimes you wonder if it would be selfish to call a suicide hotline just to say, "I can't sleep." The light of the moon taunts you until you are eventually forced to watch the sky change from black to purple to pink to orange to blue.

My insomnia diminishes when I drink enough booze to pass out. Waking up with a hangover is preferable to a night of mental anguish. I've also learned that my insomnia enhances tenfold when I accidentally overdose on a cocktail of non-FDA-approved hallucinogenic drugs provided by a very attractive and charming stranger.

I met Isaac at a Christmas party in the Lower East Side, which was predominantly attended by notable (and not-so-notable) members of the art world. He was standing in a corner alone, close to the open bar. I tend to remain close to the open bar at this sort of function. After a million free drinks, several regrettable conversations, and a bout of embarrassing solo dancing, I noticed he hadn't left his little corner.

I walked up to him and asked, "Are you here alone?"

"Yeah," he said. "Are you?"

"No, I'm with my friends." I pointed to my friends chain-smoking cigarettes out the floor-to-ceiling windows. "Have we met?"

"No, but I think we have mutual friends."

I was so drunk that I don't remember anything else we talked about but I remember wanting to kiss him. I don't remember giving him my phone number either but he contacted me the next day. "Hey, it's Isaac. I have a Droid. Sorry about the green texts." He told me he was going west for the holidays and would be back after the New Year. I suggested we hang out when he returned, to which he responded, "Absolutely." A single-word phrase I would later learn to adore.

Since I left my wallet in a cab on New Year's Eve, it was difficult to meet up with Isaac somewhere I felt comfortable, i.e., a bar. Instead I did some shots at my place and took the bus to his, taking swigs of vodka on the way. Perhaps it was irresponsible to go to a stranger's apartment while drunk but his charm was strong. He lived in a much nicer neighborhood than my own. I recognized his building immediately because my ex-boyfriend lived in the same one. The doorman was different than I'd remembered.

Isaac's living room was inviting and warm. In fact, it was so warm that I asked to crack a window and borrow a T-shirt. A few pedestrian yet endearing tempera paintings leaned against his wall. "I'm getting into painting," he said. I told him I wished I was a painter instead of a writer and he said, "Me too," because he was a poet. Apparently he told me that the night we met but I could not recall. He fixed us flat tequila sodas and we talked about our family traumas and how long we've lived in New York. He told me his parents were stamp collectors and I told him mine were Republicans. We agreed that the city sucked but we would never leave.

When my drink was finished I offered to make the second round. To my dismay, the tequila bottle was nearly empty. "Is this all the booze in your house?"

"Yeah, I can go get more if you want."

"That's OK," I lied. I didn't want to tell him I was an alcoholic.

When I finished the drink I pulled out a pack of American Spirits from my bag. "I think you should know that I'm addicted to cigarettes and a raging alcoholic."

"I had a hunch," he said. "I should probably tell you that I'm pretty into hallucinogens right now." He opened a small box on the coffee table to reveal his stash— powders, a rainbow of pills, and folded-up pieces of paper. Because he was so cute and the tequila was gone, I let him convince me to trip with him. I was afraid and had never tripped before but I was so smitten that I probably would have jumped off a bridge if he said it would be fun.

Isaac weighed out some powder and we each railed a line. About an hour passed and we didn't feel anything so we did some more. Then we swallowed some pills that were supposed to mimic the effects of MDMA. Then he kissed me. I closed my eyes and stepped into a different room in my mind. I could feel the trip getting started. When Isaac went to the bathroom I did another secret line of whatever was on the table. He returned with one of those soft baby brushes and brushed my hair as my body melted into the couch. The apartment was just the right temperature. Isaac smelled like peppermint and coconut. It was shaping up to be a perfect first date and I felt like I could possibly love him.

It's difficult to determine how much time had passed before I stood up and fell down. I couldn't feel my body so I began hitting myself in the face. Hard. "I'm not me anymore, I'm not me anymore," I repeated hysterically. "I think I'm broken. Am I broken? Did you break me, Isaac?"

"You're not broken." He put me down on the couch and restrained my arms to keep me from hitting myself. His once slender body was mutating into an alien shape. "If you're broken, everyone is going to kill me."

"I'm so scared." I tugged on my own hair. "Is this real? Am I going to die?" I closed my eyes and spiraled out of control into psychedelic planes I never had intentions of visiting, ever.

"I don't want to be in outer space." My voice was muffled and foreign. "When is this going to be over?"

"Soon," he said. His voice was unrecognizable.

He carried me to the bathroom and filled the tub with warm water. He told me not to look in the mirror so I looked in the mirror and began hitting myself again. The person in the mirror was an old, terrified woman.

She had black sunken eyes and her skin was pale gray. Her cheeks drooped down to her neck and her thin white hair was like yarn. She opened her mouth to reveal she had no teeth. That's when I started screaming.

"I don't want to be stuck like this forever. Why did you break my brain?"

Moments later I was in the tub with my clothes still on and Isaac was brushing my hair again.

The drugs were wearing off but I knew I wouldn't be able to sleep due to the severe insomnia—the perfect way to end my already terrifying and embarrassing psychedelic experience. He carried me into his bedroom, dressed me in dry clothing and tucked me into bed. The sun was coming up and his bed felt like a pile of hay. He held me while I tried forcing myself to sleep by counting his heartbeats and attempting to sync my breathing to his, but every time I closed my eyes I began to hallucinate all over again so I stared at the ceiling fan, which still did not resemble a normal ceiling fan.

"I can't sleep."

"Neither can I. Do you want to take a melatonin?"

"I can't do any more drugs. Do you think you can just roll a marble down the hallway?"

"What does that mean?"

"I don't know. I just made it up. Like, imagine rolling a marble down a really long hallway. Can you just talk to me?" I kissed his shoulder. "About anything. Nothing too intense, just something normal. Can you please do that?"

"Absolutely."

First he talked about a pizza he had made last week:

I got really into making pizzas a few months ago so I bought a marble pizza slab on Amazon. The slab changes every-thing about the pizza. It kind of cooks all of the ingredients together without losing the flavor of each individual ingredi-ent. The slab somehow keeps the heat inside of the dough so it cooks evenly. I got all of my ingredients at the food co-op. I wanted to make a pizza that I had never tried before so I got fresh pineapple and jalapeño even though I've always been skeptical of pineapple on pizza. Making the dough is the hardest part because you have to make that the night before. I guess you could buy dough from a pizza place but it isn't the same. So the next day you have to knead the dough until it's super thin. The pizza guys make it look a lot easier than it is. Dough breaks so easily. Then I made a red sauce with crushed tomatoes, tomato paste, and a bunch of spices but mostly oregano. Then I grated the cheese and cut my finger on the grater. Then I added the toppings and put it in the oven. It smelled like it was burning because the cheese was melting over the slab into the oven so I took it out to cool. It was kind of raw on the inside but I was happy with the pineapple.

Then he told me about a bizarre sandwich that you can only find in Fort Greene and what a day of working in a food co-op was like. He described the Whole Foods in his hometown and his childhood bedroom:

I had a wooden bunk bed even though I didn't share my room with my sister. Her room was next to mine. Sometimes we would talk to each other through the air vents when we both got sent to our rooms for being bad. There was dinosaur wall-paper that matched the comforter on the bottom bunk. Blue and yellow cartoon dinosaurs parading around the spread and the walls. I kept my Ninja Turtles sleeping bag on the top bunk for when my best friend, Jimmy, would sleep over. I had Thomas the Tank Engine pillowcases. Underneath the bottom bunk was a drawer where I kept all of my racecars, wooden train tracks, toy dinosaurs, and Legos. I used to give my toys to Jimmy but my parents found out and said I wasn't allowed to do that anymore. There was a dark-blue ceiling fan that I put glow-in-the-dark stars on. And I had this huge, realistic painting of a dinosaur, the one with the long neck, walking down a highway, knocking over a truck. I had a bas-ketball hoop on the back of my door so I could never close the door all the way. There was a star-shaped nightlight next to the air vent where I used to talk to my sister. I'm pretty sure the carpet was light blue but it was covered in stains.

My childhood bedroom was unicorn themed. I had a small TV on a white wicker stand on which I'd watch *Peter Pan* every night because my parents never told me bedtime stories. Sometimes my dad would wake me up in the early morning and bring me to Denny's for pancakes. He was an insomniac, too. Isaac's anecdotes were hardly bedtime stories but they felt like lullabies when his words resonated into my neck. I was still awake but I was calm and contented. It was the safest I'd felt in a really long time.

"You're pretty good at rolling marbles."

"You mean just talking endlessly about nothing?"

"Yeah, you're good at it. Maybe you should do a podcast or something, to soothe people who can't sleep. Or you could work for an Insomniacs' Hotline. Or a hotline for people who overdose on psychedelics on first dates."

It was nighttime again when we woke up, and the ceiling fan looked like a ceiling fan again. My brain felt fried but not broken. Isaac looked as beautiful as he did when we first met. He squeezed me tight and apologized for such an "intense night." I apologized for being an amateur and he said he was glad he didn't break me. I thanked him for saving me and he said it was his fault in the first place. I told him about the secret line I took while he was in the bathroom.

There are instances when you can experience simultaneous terror and magic during the span of a single night spent here on earth, but those instances are rare. I was, in that moment, no longer tripping through outer space or scared of the dark but suddenly I was afraid of something far scarier—the potential of falling in love with a stranger named Isaac.

"Can we get a mulligan?"

"What's a mulligan?" I asked.

"It's a do-over. If you really fuck up a shot in golf, you're allowed to swing again. It's called a mulligan. Let's do last night over, like a second first date. We can order a pizza and watch a movie like normal people not on drugs. Maybe we can even have consensual sex."

"Can we get a pineapple pizza?"

"Absolutely."

Noel Freibert

Peter Walked His Dog at Night

Corky's Outer-edge was a delicate area, a space where anything could happen, a fertile wound of land open to infection. Neither private nor public, it was the place at the sidewalk's edge where the street dead-ended. In the beginning, Corky noticed that debris congregated there. Like a metal cylinder reading "Pepsi-Cola" in cold aluminum script. Napkins and bags would appear as if sprouted from the ground. Once an advertisement from Stromboli's Express decomposed on the grass, "Quality & Convenience." Sometimes house pets passed beyond the Outer-edge, teasing the boundary of the subdivision. A pet could transcend over the sidewalk's boundary, thought to be dead, and then return unannounced, as if nothing was amiss.

Corky returned one once. "Your cat is no longer a cat, Ms. Sauerbeck." Ms. Sauerbeck took the animal back. She didn't hear or believe that anything in it had changed. Her mistake.

Corky's house looked like all the others in Forest Springs. Her window faced out toward the sidewalk, toward the houses across the street. Blank American structures, identical except for a flair of color here, an ornamental bush there. The one with the manicured hedges, the one precisely across the street, that was Peter's house. His bedroom window faced her bedroom window directly. On this night all of the lights in Peter's house were out, there was nothing for Corky to see. It made the night seem even darker as she squinted and scanned, trying to catch any detail unavailable. On nights like this Corky sometimes wished that Peter would look out at her and offer an inviting glance. She longed for some kind of window-to-window gesture, a connection, something to brighten this black suburban night.

In daylight, the Outer-edge was visible from Corky's bedroom window. Corky thought of herself as the guardian of the edge. To her dismay, not a lot went on there at the end of the sidewalk.

"... not yet anyway," Corky whispered under her breath.

Over the past three years, since she was a freshman, Corky had taken it upon herself to maintain her Outer-edge, the overgrown area where her street dead-ended. She couldn't do much about the thicker growth, but she took pride in pulling up weed sprouts and disposing of debris as it appeared.

Anything to keep the neighborhood safe, Corky thought.

Some of the weeds in Corky's edge had grown there since before her parents moved to the subdivision. To her dismay she couldn't do a thing about them. One particular elder weed had developed into a tree sturdy enough to climb. This was the growth that most con-cerned her. On more than one occasion she tried to peel its bark off, hoping it would die of exposed innards. The bark always grew back stronger, sometimes with areas scabbed over, oozing thick with sap. She cherished any sign of pain she could evoke. She imagined the growth, the elder weed-tree, as an inappropriate body. It was an alien from beyond the Outer-edge. Her efforts surely prevented its ambient intrusion into her closed-gate community. Corky smiled as the tree bled out.

On this night the old weed-tree couldn't have been fur-ther from Corky's mind. Tonight she was fixated on Peter. Perched at her bedroom window she imagined a few weeks ago when she saw him more regularly, back when Trin was still alive. Corky used to spot Peter in the late afternoon for his routine dog walk. Slyly studying by the window, Corky would wait for his appearance, never letting on to her parents her true desire, to observe her neighborly crush.

She imagined him, Peter, with his blonde shaggy hair, tan skin, and his dog Trin (short for Trinity) by his side. Corky didn't know the dog's exact name; Trinity was a name she made up until she learned of the dog's proper name. Trin was a well-mannered Golden Lab. She never needed the leash, but Peter would always carry it, wrapped taught around his wrist, just in case. Corky admired Peter's path. He took his walks toward the west side of the neighborhood, away from her Outer-edge. He was such a good guy. She knew it from his style, posture, and direction. There was a nerve inside of her that wished he might walk the opposite way for once, toward the sidewalk's end. A fantasy that she might be able to show off her area to him, no matter how unstable it seemed sometimes.

Corky's desires flooded the blank suburban night. Perched at her window longing for Peter, Corky witnessed something unexpected. A bright wave over the manicured lawn, the motion sensor light at the front of Peter's house flicked on. Excitement filled Corky.

There was a long moment of stillness. Corky began to wonder if the motion sensor might've been set off by a squirrel or a drifting leaf. She looked deeply around the edges of the sensor's beam. Something was there. Some kind of movement in the shadows. Corky's body became still, pressed up against the glass. There, indistinct, a sketch of a figure.

"Who's there?"

Corky pressed firmly against the window to soak up any possible detail.

Weeks ago Corky had heard from her parents that the neighbors' dog had been "put down." She wished she had known Peter better, she might have been able to console him. She could only imagine how the loss of a companion must've felt.

Perplexed by the vague figure in the recess of Peter's lawn, Corky's mind wandered. Without a dog to take out, what might this figure be up to? She had never seen her neighbors out this late before. Not Peter, not his parents. They had always kept quite regular hours, Corky thought.

As she peered into the blank stillness, details gradually emerged. Corky's mind raced. A late-night trash removal? Odd day of the week for that activity, Corky thought.

Then a slow revelation. A limb emerged into the perimeter of light.

"Uh, uh, a limb!" Corky thought. "Er, it's an arm!"

An arm of slender young white flesh with something tethered around it. Corky squinted, begged her eyes to recognize the shape.

Some constraint about the wrist of it. A dark mass was tied around the arm.

A flash of recognition as her brain decoded the shape. What was being illuminated was an arm decorated by the coil of a dog's leash.

Corky gasped, her breath making a shape on the cold glass.

It must be Peter out on some midnight task, Corky thought, trying to move her mind from the unsettling question at hand. He must be running a misplaced errand or maybe he's going for a jog, restless from the passing of Trin. Corky's mind flew to find an excuse for the midnight sighting.

The tethered arm in the cold sensor's light revealed what it was appendaged to, a pallid torso, sunken in the center, the ribs protruding. Then the neck and waist came into view. Lengthened as if distraught from a lack of nourishment. Yet another arm and two legs emerged into the light. A famished form of pale loose skin. The body was nude except for a slinking boxer brief haphazardly about the middle. Then the feet appeared, paws of upright human flesh. The body looked like a foreign object, but who else would wear a dog's leash in such a fashion, taut around the wrist? Finally, the head entered the illuminated place and the identity was confirmed. Peter's body stood there. Its shadow, a terrible shaking form, elongated the features even further into the black bag of the night.

The body of Peter rested, momentarily paused in the bath of bright light. Then with slow agony it moved, step by step, in a new direction.

Corky was unsure at to what most concerned her about the scene—the dire state of the body, the leash worn without purpose, or the direction the figure lumbered toward. The body limped down the driveway and then due east toward the end of the sidewalk, toward Corky's Outer-edge.

Flushed in panic Corky gripped her Claremont High hoodie. Without thinking, she lowered herself from her bedroom window and entered the blank, black suburban night. In the distance Corky struggled to locate the shrinking form of Peter's body. The sensor light of his house continued to shine, but his shape was nowhere to be found.

"What will I say to him?" Corky wondered. "We've never even spoken, what a fucked-up way to meet my crush."

Unsure, Corky began pacing down in the direction Peter had departed, toward the sidewalk's end, her Outer-edge. Her mind darted to the dire potential that her encounter might hold, given the time and place.

What if Peter has moved beyond the subdivision's boundary? What will I tell his parents? Corky felt a responsibility alongside her desire for Peter.

Her heart raged as her feet pounded the sidewalk. Her mind went away, her thoughts evaporated, Corky became a running mass bent to a purpose, to find the body of Peter.

Her eyes noticed something out there, as she approached the vicinity of the Outer-edge. Something white floated above the blackened ground. She thought she had cleaned up all of the debris from today, but perhaps not. Something visible was attached to the tree of her contempt.

Corky struggled to make out the form. She stalled, cautious of her surroundings, yet compelled to witness the sight ahead in its fully dim detail.

"Oh god, not there, anywhere but the tree," Corky thought.

Her drawn-out approach slowly unveiled the scene of her desires.

"Could it really be him?" she thought as she moved ever closer.

The pale object floated in the distance, about where her dreaded weed-tree stood. The white shape drifted slightly, left to right. Corky's eyes adjusted, pupils opened wider to suck in all the faded light.

There they swayed, Peter's slender pale arms, but the dog's leash had gone missing.

"It must've abandoned the body along the path," she thought.

Confused by the slow realization, she began to more acutely recognize the details of the floating body. The same shape from before, the same arms, the same sunken chest, the same waisted boxers, the stretched-out legs, the knees floated near Corky's face. The heels of the feet brushed against the tree's sappy scab.

"Peter, it's your neighbor Corky. You OK?"

Her eyes slowly perceived the face. Peter stared down at Corky's feet, mouth gaping open.

"What're you doing? Need some help?"

His expression was bland, his face had let go of its composure. Corky stared into his eyes to try to connect with him.

"Can you hear me?"

Then she noticed it. The collar of the dog's leash wrapped around Peter's neck. A rare detail in the dim night. Her eyes followed the trail of the leash to where Peter had tied the opposite end to the firmest of the weed-tree's branches. His body dangled there, lifelessly floating. He had hanged himself from the weed. Corky's mind struggled. She backed away. Then turned to sprint.

Back in her room Corky pressed on her eyes, an attempt to erase the memory.

"Peter went over the Outer-edge tonight," Corky thought, "he's fallen through the suburb's seam, wandering somewhere beyond." She knew he'd never find his way back.

Some weeks later a boy wandered down to the sidewalk's end. He saw something dangling from a tree. It was a strange growth as if a bundle of sticks and long rocks had been wrapped in a rotting bag.

Corky told no one of her midnight experience. The body became a fruit of the weed. Another alien blossom that plagued Corky's mind.

Peter was not there.

Plates

Bad Cat, 2018
Foam, velvet, epoxy, steel, plastic,
enamel paint, thread, zipper, hardware
141 × 173 × 68 inches

A Man With (and Without) Glasses, 2018
Acrylic paint, poplin, sequin pins,
foam, velvet, hardware, wood, plexiglass
96 × 96 × 3½ inches

Bad Break (II), 2018
Plexiglass, vinyl film, vinyl siding, plywood,
epoxy clay, laminate, house paint, hardware
72 × 72 × 4 inches

Slow Web, 2018
Neon, vinyl siding, laminate, plywood,
epoxy clay, house paint, hardware
72 × 72 × 4 inches

Double Vision, 2018
Neon, vinyl siding, laminate, plywood,
epoxy clay, house paint, hardware
72 × 72 × 4 inches

Good Window with Candle (Purple), 2018
Neon, vinyl siding, laminate, plywood,
epoxy clay, house paint, hardware
72 × 86 × 6 inches

Bad Breeze (II), 2018
Neon, vinyl siding, laminate, plywood,
epoxy clay, house paint, hardware
72 × 72 × 6 inches

Hot Pie, 2018
Neon, vinyl siding, laminate, plywood,
epoxy clay, house paint, hardware
72 × 79 × 6 inches

Bad Breeze (III), 2018
Neon, vinyl siding, laminate, plywood,
epoxy clay, house paint, hardware
72 × 72 × 6 inches

Night Vision, 2018
Neon, vinyl siding, laminate, plywood,
epoxy clay, house paint, motorized
Halloween prop eyeballs, Arduino board,
hardware
72 × 72 × 6 inches

Bad Window with Wood, 2018
Neon, vinyl siding, laminate, plywood,
epoxy clay, house paint, hardware
72 × 72 × 4 inches

The Open Window, 2018
HD digital video, sound
11 minutes, 1 second

Sam McKinniss

Hell Means Never Having to Say You're Sorry

"How would you define vice?" some nerd asked from out of nowhere. Sam never even saw him coming. It was a dark and stormy night, which, normally, Sam preferred. He loved the dark and didn't mind the rain. Light made everything visible, terrifying and large. In Sam's estimation, lack of sunlight was kinder, gentler ... but now this. This nerd must have spied Sam from the rear corner booth before getting up and zeroing in like some kind of nonsexual predator. Had Sam known he was in the room, adequate precautions could have been taken, contingencies prepped, this little run-in might have been cut off at the pass or avoided altogether.

But Sam ran into this guy a lot, actually, at bars or parties, and he never seemed to remember his name, however he did have a memorable face. Fish-shaped with pallid coloring and humongous, oddly shaped eyeballs on either side of his head. Tepid brown hair, incapable of shock or volume. A lot of amphibian nonsense in the form of an adult human male. Too tall, also, so Sam had to look up whenever this fishy dork deigned to talk down to him. Contrary to the declaration emblazoned across his T-shirt, geeks didn't stand a chance of inheriting the earth. He was a real know-it-all, with credentials completely unbeknownst to Sam or perhaps anybody, he just showed up in places like this and started asking stupid questions. And here he was at Sam's local bar, god, does he live around here? Fuck. He drinks here? Shit.

"That's an interesting question, I'm so glad you asked. Vice is difficult to define, but I guess I'll take a stab at it. I work for myself. I'm trying to relax here, maybe you knew that. That doesn't mean I'm not happy to see you, I'm just a little worn out. I came from work, which was just me, by myself, you know, just paying myself all day long. I'm kidding, I don't know if I made any money today. I'm an artist, I'm sure you knew that. And I am my own boss, that part is true. I have to put the paintbrush down several times a day to get on the phone and yap at somebody to make sure I'm being paid enough to live or otherwise negotiate my best interests with the various galleries consigning my paintings to the extent that everyone is willing and able to work together. Is that OK with you? I don't want to get into details right now, the art world is shrouded in mystery. Anyway, when six or seven o'clock rolls around I feel like I've earned the right to take myself out for a few drinks and stew over how much I hate my boss. Which like I just said is me. I hate myself. Actually, I like myself, I just hate being alive. I'd love to unwind one day, I really would.

"Moving on and to answer your question, if both of us are willing to agree that independence is a virtue, and I think we are, then we ought to be ready to define vice as the opposite of virtue, at which point we might want to describe the opposite of independence as dependence. So you see where I'm going with this. In order to balance out the staggering success of my small business, relying on myself to make art all fucking day long, well, I've developed an alcohol dependency. It's a yin-yang kind of thing. It takes the edge off. Fuck I love that about alcohol. Look, I don't mean to be rude, but my wedding ring fell off about twenty minutes ago and I have to go look for it." Sam turned around, rolled his eyes, and walked back to the bar; his glass was empty. He hadn't been married in about two years, but the ring gag was still valid with people who didn't know any better, and fish-nerd did not have the right.

"Elton John called, he wants to know if you can feel the love tonight."

"Do you want another dark 'n' stormy, Sam?"

"Yes."

Dante mixed him another cocktail. Dark 'n' stormys were the only drink Sam ever ordered. He liked a tequila or two on special occasions, but special occasions were likewise difficult to define. Part of the reason Sam preferred dark 'n' stormys is because they are delicious, but more importantly because it only takes about forty-five seconds to mix one. That means less time waiting around to be served and being served is the best, case closed. Sam figured that out at age sixteen when he used to swap IDs with his straight-edge older brother to go drinking at the bars near their childhood home, five years ahead of schedule. His older brother never noticed the swapped-out ID scam and neither for some reason did any of the local barmen, even though Sam's voice still hadn't dropped at that point from its soaring teenage soprano.

Dante had curly brown shoulder-length hair and big smiling eyes. Articulate little hands and fingers, nails neatly trimmed. He faced his work with alacrity, a friend to all who entered the bar. He was always stoned. The strain of marijuana he preferred rendered him soft spoken and amenable to servility, though it was obvious that periodically Dante felt that something was missing, something he very desperately wanted instead. While engaging in routine barroom conversation, Sam had noticed sudden, painful squints in Dante's eyes every now and then, or else, two lips turned down into split-second frowns. An aura hung about him that specified a truth to his circumstance, namely, that Dante would rather be anyplace else, taking his clothes off, watching TV, and smoking tons of weed in the nude.

"Thanks," Sam took the drink and laid seven singles out on the bar and waited for Dante to pick them up before laying down another dollar for tip. Dante winked and moved on to some other loner. Enough time had passed since the night a few weeks ago when Sam had sucked Dante off in a bathroom stall after closing down the bar. Things between them had calmed down finally to a point where the two of them were behaving as if nothing had happened. It didn't even matter, in Sam's opinion; it was just another expression of Sam's heartfelt appreciation for Dante, fellatio between two consenting adult men, but perhaps meant as a more robust tip from Sam, more generous than the customary single dollar bill per beverage.

Sam really was alone now, plenty of space between him and the nerd, enough time between his and Dante's moment of bathroom passion, alone while he waited for literally anyone to join him. Which was fine. Sam loved drinking alone in front of Dante, sneaking in a few laughs and then wandering off by himself into the night under streetlamps. Sam had been hanging out in this bar regularly for quite a while even, before Dante started working there. And then when Dante showed up, forget about it. No other bar compared.

Suddenly Sam's phone vibrated, alerting him to a phone call from Satan.

"Oh fuck, Satan's in town," said Sam.

He picked up. "What is this, a phone call?" People ought to just text, Sam thought.

"Hahaha, it's me. Hi Sam. Do you want to get a drink?"

"I thought I made that clear to you months ago. Of course I want a drink. I'm at the bar."

"Oh right, haha, of course. OK, well, I'll swing by. I'd like to see you. I'm in the neighborhood."

Satan was, for lack of a better way of saying it, the man in Sam's life. They'd been on intimate terms for about a year at that point, off and on. Mostly off, but the on times had been so intense, and had happened at such regular intervals, involving depths of emotion so shamefully embarrassing, Sam had had trouble getting Satan out of his head. All of Sam's friends hated him, believing he was suspicious and generally up to no good, but that didn't matter to Sam. When Satan came calling, Sam was powerless to resist.

For starters, Satan was hot. Like unbelievably handsome. Clothes clung to his rock-hard body as if hanging on for dear life. He was charming, intelligent, witty, a smooth conversationalist. And nobody else as far as Sam ever knew could fuck like Satan fucked. Having sex with Satan was like being hit by a car, but instead of dying you became blessed with the knowledge of profound right and wrong, awakening internal organs, physical talents, and the capacity to dream in big, lurid detail, stuff you never even knew existed becoming fruitful and multiplying, filling the earth with copious semen.

And they had done that a lot. They first met at a candlelit dinner party held many moons ago by a since-disgraced member of the film industry, some defiler of women they'd both happened to barely know at all. Satan looked deep into Sam's furtive eyes from across the table, seated there via fateful accident. After a little decorous small talk, Satan established unbreakable eye contact with Sam and ravished his innermost desires like so many open secrets. They bailed on dessert and went back to Sam's place. From that night on, life transformed into an appalling test of endurance, waiting and waiting for Satan to visit again in the fullness of temptation and pleasure, enrapturing him from the brink of wretched meantime spent near death and without him.

"Dante, I'm going to need another drink, Satan's on his way here."

"Really? I didn't know you guys were still together. Are you guys boyfriends or something?"

"I don't know how to answer that question."

"I'm not sure I like him for you, I've only met him a few times but he's kind of a shady character, if you don't mind my saying so."

"Look, I know that already, a lot of people keep telling me that, but you know what? The heart wants what it wants, and right now mine wants two things: another dark 'n' stormy and for Satan to fuck me later."

Dante poured ginger beer over rum and ice before garnishing it all with a lime wedge. Satan entered the bar undetected, hung his black leather cloak on a hook near the door and kissed Sam on the back of the neck. Thrills shot down Sam's spine like a bomb raid.

"Oh my god," Sam gasped.

"No, just me," replied Satan. Sam turned around, smiled, and kissed him hello on the lips.

"What'll it be, Satan?" asked Dante, dutiful as ever.

"Tequila on the rocks with a splash of soda and lime, thanks."

"How are you?" asked Sam.

"I've been well, just busy. It's nice to see you."

"Likewise, Satan, you know I love seeing you. It's been a while. You look great. I thought maybe you'd gotten sick of me. Last time we saw each other, I was a bit of a mess, sorry for becoming so maudlin that night. I don't know if you remember. Unfortunately I remember all of it."

"At this point, I think we're beyond apologies. We've seen each other in many different lights, you know, some of them rather unflattering. But you can't offend me. You don't ever need to apologize to me," offered Satan. He was capable of expressing a level of high-mindedness so advanced that even Sam couldn't help but find it irritating.

"But one ought to, don't you think? I mean, good grief, it's a nice thing to do, after I dragged you out of that party, yelling at you like that and then crying, I mean we were on a street corner in fucking Chinatown at two in the morning and I fucking cried and yelled at you about us, or about what are we doing. I mean it didn't feel like me, although of course it was classic behavior on my part, as we are well aware. I'm sure you didn't enjoy that."

Scenes like the one in Chinatown had been a fairly consistent feature of the relationship. The only thing that seemed to change was location. Chinatown could just as easily have been Chelsea, or Los Angeles, or Paris, or Helsinki for that matter, wherever Satan had business, beckoning Sam to come join him. Satan plied Sam for romantic evenings out on the town, and sometimes for days on end with promises of a good time. Sam didn't even know what kind of business Satan was in. Whatever it was, he was very often able to procure impossibly difficult-to-find concert tickets, four-night stays in five-star hotels, rare steaks and good wine without effort, all before inevitably getting drunk and stumbling into long arguments about the eventual unlikelihood of love between them or any flavor of commitment, difficulties arising from both of their natural disinclinations to either of those things, despite the urgency of Sam's response to the other's slick overtures. The attraction was there, so too were opportunities to act on it, but Sam often wondered if Satan had a soul. What usually followed was more pondering about what was happening to his.

"Oh I don't care, I just hate seeing you like that. You know our friendship is important to me. I love hanging out with you, you're excellent company. I just can't be anyone's boyfriend. I thought we were on the same page. I've said that to you before, Sam, countless times. I can't be your boyfriend. I am so emotionally unavailable, I'm not even in touch with *myself* most of the time. It's impossible at this point in my life to be anything more than a close friend to you. I am fond of you, though, you know that. Want a bump?" Satan produced a vial of cocaine from somewhere on his person, and filled a long pinky fingernail with powder. He sniffed it up, refilled his scooplike nail and let it hover just below Sam's nose.

"I don't see why not." Sam snorted it. Satan always had great drugs, another item on the list of things he had going for him. "Oh my, how nice. I don't know how you always find such fantastic cocaine. My goodness, do you want another drink? I seem to have finished mine." Jazzed up on narcotized infallibility, Sam waved at Dante.

There was nothing else to talk about, but that wouldn't stop them from ordering more spirits to loose the magic of chitchat out from their tongues. Satan was in the neighborhood that night, and so for reasons too mysterious for anyone to discern, it was necessary for the Prince of Darkness to check in on bright, beautiful Sam. But being "in the neighborhood" was nothing more than a convenient lie to tell. Satan already knew where Sam was, always knew exactly what he was up to. Sam never had any secrets. Everyone had his number. He was

America's Sweetheart. There wasn't anyone who didn't know absolutely everything about him. At any given time, every single person on the planet already knew what his heart most desired. And not only that, they all cared. Everybody was rooting for him. It was absurd, really, and a tad grandiose, but that's how it was. Satan's omniscient telepathic powers aside (which by the way have been somewhat overstated, historically speaking), Sam was predictable, and he projected. He was out there following his heart. In doing so, he couldn't help but broadcast his intentions to a vast, worldwide community of believers, an audience rapt, on the edges of their seats at all times. And why did they all care so much? They wanted to know if America's Sweetheart would ever find love and hold on to it.

In terms of where to find *him*, if he wasn't at a museum opening reception, a gallery dinner, or after-party pretending to celebrate some weirdo's latest artistic achievement, you could find Sam drinking at one of like three bars in New York. It was true that Satan enjoyed flying him to lavish destinations around the world on sex-filled weekend getaways, who wouldn't? But he also liked sneaking up on him from behind corners at random downtown functions, just to freak him out a little bit. Sam spooked easily. It was fun.

They sat there engrossed in drink for three more hours before Sam slipped and fell off his barstool. Maybe he had tried standing up and then tripped on a rung, what-ever. He was now, suddenly, laid out flat on his back and cursing. The fall made quite a commotion, sounds of furniture crashing and a thud, followed by an uncomfort-able hush spread thick across the room. Other patrons were startled, and then of course they were gravely con-cerned. Here was America's Sweetheart, piss drunk and swearing loudly on the floor. "Oh my god, is he OK?" some frantic stranger yelled in the background. Satan looked down at him before calmly finishing the last of his tequila. It wasn't the first time he'd seen him like this.

"Oh dear, I guess he's had too much to drink, should I call him a cab, Satan? We need to get him on his feet," said Dante, weariness or exasperation now evident on the edge of his voice.

"No, that's alright, I'm parked out front. I'm good to drive. He'll be fine with me."

Fish-nerd rushed over to see what the fuss was about. Satan flashed him a sinister glare, shooing him away. Then he descended from atop his stool, knelt down and wrapped arms around Sam. Flush with booze and the tenderness of defeat, Sam reached around and slid hands down Satan's backside, taking hold of his soft, powerful haunches. He let out a tiny drunken whimper. "It seems to me you live your life like a candle in the wind, Sam."

"Shut up. I'm sorry but I am very drunk. What were we talking about? What are we going to do now?"

"I thought I told you, never apologize. Come on, let's get you to bed."

"You're such a nice guy, Satan, I don't know why all my friends think you're so evil."

"Well, I guess that's just my cross to bear."

Satan scooped him up like a corpse, carried him out the front door, and settled him into the passenger's seat of his ride. And then they were off, under cover of darkness.

Sarah Nicole Prickett

Jack Hansom Gets the Blues

The studios on Pearl Street had been a warehouse, and the painter who worked on the fifth floor, end of the hall, liked to say that it remained a place for tools. He hated the late conceptualists invading the ground floor. He hated the rusty sculptors on second and the unskilled, shameless appropriators on third. Jack Hansom was thirty-eight years old and would never be famous. He didn't look like a worker, but he dressed like one in blue denim overalls and white T-shirts, shipped twelve to a box from Lands' End, and white plimsoll sneakers. His Papa's Seiko had been broken for years.

Sun said it was noon. Corners burst with bottles, bags from the deli. Cracked jars of paint stood mid-leak. Every few feet a mirror leaned insolently against the wall, catching the rays and scattering them over older, smaller paintings. Seven new ones patched the dilapidating white brick walls. Each a good sixty by eighty inches. He was using bedsheets now, where the other guys, suckers, were still on canvas. Jack Hansom could finish a painting three days before a show and it'd be dry by hanging time.

Or was it two days before? His opening was Friday, as the girls up at the gallery had phoned to remind him twice. He remembered it being Sunday, just the other day. He'd had the steak at Bastille. That didn't solve the problem of what day it was today.

The machine blinked. Message about a bill from Pearl Paint, ninety days due but since when. Message from Darling to let him know about "dinner on Thursday." Another message from the art-reporter chick at the *Village Voice* who called every two to three days, wanting an interview on the pretense that it was "his year," that he was "getting his due." He never answered. This time she asked nothing, only said she was excited to see the new work. Maybe this chick had finally been hit with the news that he didn't do press. Her last words were staticky, then "tomorrow." He rewound and played it again, short of breath. Yes, "tomorrow."

Jack Hansom thought for the first time that he might have a problem, because it was the first time he'd considered that after days without sleep, his opening might be tomorrow. His wife had made plans for tonight. And he was out of amphetamines.

Sharp, loud knock on the door. He startled, then exhaled relief. Tuesdays and only Tuesdays were for deliveries. For once he wanted to hear the delivery guy try to be cute, say exaggeratedly, "Yepppppp. Tuesday again."

When he opened the door it was a girl and she wasn't dressed like a guy.

"Hello," said the girl. "Are you the artist?"

Sure, he thought. Like any real artist would answer. She must mean one of the pseuds downstairs.

"Wrong unit," he said.

She looked left down the corridor, then right around his shoulder into the space.

"Not expecting me, huh." A slight grin. "They said at the gallery you'd forget. I *did* leave a message."

"Here?"

"Here. I mean, if here is where Jack Hansom keeps his phone."

On the machine her voice had been cooler and dilatory, like water in the morning from a clotted pipe. Here her idiolect glinted. Her bright, rushing laugh made him want to talk. He tried to remember her name, whether she'd left it on the last message. Let alone when he could have agreed to this.

"What day is it?"

"It's the day," she said. "And not only is it the day, but it's the time."

He remembered the name being plain and old-fashioned, like Anna or Sandra. Sarah maybe. Everything else about the girl repudiated plainness. Green eyes, stippled with puce. Hair tinted an alarming shade of red, tumbling in fitful waves to a pair of shoulders so straight they looked hung from her neck with a level. On the right side her nose too was straight and her jaw almost square. On the left her profile was longer and awry. He wouldn't say pretty, exactly. She had a face that made symmetry irrelevant, bones angled significantly, mouth palpable, the eyes matched and gleaming like a hot pair of gemstones in an open palm.

He opened the door wider.

Ten minutes later the red-haired girl hadn't said a word. He sat on an iron barstool with hairpin legs, watching her in the up-angled mirrors. He liked her movements about the space. Thighs perspiring in a miniskirt of cool green suede, feet light in gold metallic jazz shoes, bits of Canal Street gold jangling on her wrist. She jotted things down in a memo book. He kept forgetting to offer her tea, coffee.

Now she was talking. It seemed to her that painting burgers, as he'd begun doing recently, was "either hammy or cheesy." She said an older painting of Vaseline in a jar with the label on struck her as "very bad." She explained that "bad" meant "sick" and "sick" meant "good." After a while she noted that three of the ten dames in his new and recent paintings had blue hair in lieu of blonde, which would strike anyone as unusual. He waited for her to use question marks.

A painting he had not been able to finish was the first to really seize her attention. She stood at length, motionless except for a foot arched and naked in its shoe, toe tracing loops on the hardwood. The air and the light had stilled too so all that glittered was dust.

Something in the range of his heart approached, and began to speed past, dread.

"I knew someone," the girl was saying, "who had blue

hair, and brown eyes that looked blackish, and the palest skin in the world, so pale you could see her blue veins. She would have seemed easy to paint. She wasn't—I mean, it was kind of her thing, to not make anything easy."

She stopped to turn half from the painting, revealing in profile the long upward drift of her lashes, patterned after the flight of a gull, and the dusted peach of her cheek. Unbound by a bra, her nipple bobbed up on the medium swell under the silk. A quick breath, then her voice very clear.

She said: "Celia."

He tried to say nothing.

He said: "Celia?"

"Means heavenly," said the girl. "Which is to say—speaking of blue."

She turned all the way to stand straight with her back to the tall canvas, as if she were donating the piece to a museum and had prepared a short speech. She began.

"We met as waitresses. Cocktail. Downtown. It was my idea. I said if we really wanted to get paid under the table, we'd go home with the customers. I dropped out of journalism school and did nothing except see different men, but Celia went to art school, you know, and she ... had better ideas. Celia had better ideas than any girl I ever met. Imagine my surprise when she fell in love. I warned her. I said that any man who puts you through art school is not going to let you be the artist when it comes to the end."

Her speech was becoming mannered. Slower now.

"Celia was a photographer. She made self-portraits. She said, *I can afford myself.* Well, this man could more than afford her, because he was a painter and painting was back. That's what he said. Rich people believed in him. He wanted the only portraits of her to be ... *his.*"

Words rubbed in like gold leaf on an elaborate wooden frame.

"She showed me one. He drew her in pastels in one of her own notebooks and tore out the sheet, making it worthless to anyone but her. I wanted to throw it in the trash, but I couldn't. He'd gotten her look. How did he do it?"

He wanted to explain. That was how they nailed you, detectives in the movies. They appealed to the require-ment for genius, the hundredth-percentile nature of the thing, the ego it took. He wanted to say no one had his talent. He wanted to say, name one other artist who could get the look of that blue-headed girl, a seraph hallucinated on mushrooms, a changeling. There was no other artist.

The redhead was doing some explaining of her own. When Celia was found like that, the police went to her place and pretended to do their jobs. They found an address book with lots of men's names, none of them real. A half-bottle of sleeping pills with the label rubbed off. A little pot. They didn't see anything special about that little painting. They left it pinned to the wall by her bed. "It's still there," she said. "I sleep there now."

He was just going to say one thing.

"On Baxter Street. Across from the cops."

"Exactly," she said.

A mutually unfriendly gaze transpired.

"Well," he said, "I should consider myself lucky you're writing about me, because you can really tell a story. And now I guess you better ask some questions."

"You guess. I've guessed enough."

Then she laughed or began to laugh and quickly changed her mind. Mouth softened, shoulders slipping a bit from the horizontal, she moved closer and sat, like a damp chemise peeled off and dropped instead of folded, into his favourite blue chair.

"I'll get you that coffee," he said, just as though she had asked. He got up and went to the open kitchen, and began to pull out drawers, bang about. "What do you take, cream? A little sugar? A little brandy might be for the best."

Her gaze was elsewhere.

How he did it was, he made his own pigments. He liked especially to make a virulent shade of Prussian blue, and when people asked what it was about his blues, he said it was nothing. They were obvious, dumb blues. A man's blues. He would never now explain how iron mixes with hydrogen cyanide, how slowly it develops to make a hue stronger than velvet. The vial was in a shoebox, the shoebox on the highest shelf. He fumbled noisily as he could, expressing no care. She still wasn't looking. He checked the label twice to make sure.

When he brought her the cup, the color returned to her face like a memory of triumph or embarrassment, so sudden it made him almost spill. She looked at him then through wet blackened lashes. Green of her eyes turning lambent, neon-bright. He tried to see the discrepancies in her face.

"It's bitter," he said, being nice. "I can't find the sugar."

"It's fine."

As if for the first time in years he felt himself smiling. She took a brief, untasting sip and then a long one. He went back to the deep steel sink and found his mug, washed it in cold running water, with hand soap.

A loud, choking scream. A choked nothing. The gold bracelets tinkling indifferently for six, seven seconds, and outside the train rattling by.

It was easy to take her down in the freight elevator, wrapped in a drop cloth and a thirty-six by seventy-two canvas, the way he sometimes took paintings that were not going to be masterpieces and rolled them up and put them out by the dumpster. She wasn't more than thirty inches at her shoulders, and thirty-three at her hips. It was easy to put her in the bed of his ancient white pick-up, to line her side with bricks so she wouldn't roll around. It was no trouble at all getting from the West Side to Baxter Street in the middle of the afternoon, well after lunch and before rush hour, only the tourists in sun-visors out on Canal. It was a little trouble getting up the stairs. A mustachioed fishmonger passed him on the second landing, and seemed to peer into the top of the canvas roll, but then said only that it was a hot day to be redecorating up there.

Four keys materialized in the bottom of the girl's little purse, a Chinese red silk pouch with a gold-plated bamboo handle, also containing lipstick, a jade compact, a business card from the *Voice*, and a penknife. The first key he tried opened sesame. It was easy to unwrap her and lay her out on a proper bed this time, on a rose-printed spread. It was easy like that to frame her as someone he'd loved.

There was a bottle of vodka in the freezer, and it would be easy, too, to tear off a piece of his T-shirt and dip it in the vodka and wipe off his fingerprints from everywhere, and take the rag home with the rest of him and his drop cloth and canvas, and paint until sundown. He had always said he painted because it was easier than working.

Only when he remembered how close he had come to explaining his work, his process, did his palms mist up. Jack Hansom never explained. He was the artist, and explanations were fatal to the art.

On the radio in the truck he'd heard it was only Tuesday. Now a Bobby Brown song was in his head and he couldn't help singing:

> *All these strange relationships*
> *Really gets me down*
> *I see nothin' wrong*
> *With spreadin, myself around …*

Detectives and critics liked imagining motives as complex, or at the very least deep. Greed was a good one,
or passion. Lust would suffice. Boredom was only cited
by psychos, so it really meant evil or insanity. He personally did not believe in either. Crime in his mind was
quite simple, having little to do with the complicated
subject of desire. No one woke up and heard the birds
sing and smelled the coffee and thought, what I want
to do today is rob a bank, or rape someone, or kill. No,
what happened was that you had two choices, and the
easier choice happened to be criminal. It's easier not to
ask, so you rape. It's easier not to explain about a girl to
your sterile, heiress wife, so when the girl won't let you
leave her, you leave her for dead.

There was one bit of trouble. This redhead's work. As
in, this red-haired Dana or Barbara had some shmucky
editor who would know where she was going, and would
be expecting her copy pronto. When the copy failed to
materialize, the editor would phone and the phone would
ring and ring. Or an aspiring boyfriend would come over
to help her procrastinate. Or the landlord would come
to collect. But it would be the editor who'd tell the cops
that the last thing he knew, the girl was doing an interview with a painter by the name of Jack Hansom.

Maybe there was a way to change the time of death, and
by changing the time to change the place, and by changing the place to change what happened. How stupidly

she'd arranged all this to happen in his space. The high floor, thick walls. No one heard. He sighed. These down-town writers never think past their deadlines.

Yes, there was a way, and there was the electric type-writer, its color the green of Castelvetrano olives. He poured a little of the vodka into a white teacup etched with jade-green swallows and sat in the white rattan chair at the white wood desk.

He started typing. A thousand words should do it.

May 8, 1989

If a young Betsy Bloomingdale went to an orgy and got fucked by Jasper Johns, Robert Rauschenberg, Leo Burnett, Warhol, Cézanne, Ray Kroc, and the alien played by Jeff Goldblum in *Earth Girls Are Easy*, the result would be the painter Jack Hansom, whose new show, *Lies*, opens at the Little Gallery this week. Though you couldn't call him a lovechild, the bastard at heart is romantic: The formal properties of his paintings marry haste, as in his skilled, quick, and self-consciously lazy brushwork, with an irredeemable longing toward jou-issance, as evinced by certain new paintings, based on the paperback covers of trashy romances, in which a man and a woman kiss with more sincerity and wonder than any two figures in art's history have kissed since Pygmalion and Galatea.

A shaft of noon light fell over the bed, narrowly missing the sketch of Celia still pinned there. He wasn't sure about "jouissance," or whether a girl, titian or no, was allowed to say "fucked." He'd gotten the date wrong.

May 9, 1989

Jack Hansom, one of the more perverse artists of our generation, has begun painting his trashy, romanticized figures on bedsheets, as if begging for his wonderful work, already so sincere that it is dismissed as "commercial," to be called unclean. His new show, opening Friday, is bound to be a sleeper hit.

Too clever? He lit a cigarette. Tried again.

May 9, 1989

Jack Hansom, the most perverse artist of our generation, is getting his due.

Tommy Brewer

The Navy Yard

I was trying to spend every Saturday painting in the studio. My stalled art career had recently shown a pulse; I'd been included in a couple group shows, and had a studio visit scheduled with a respectable Zurich gallerist—a prospect my boyfriend, himself an art dealer, thought promising.

I was working on a new body of paintings that used a bright, figurative style, reminiscent of children's illustration, to depict psychological turmoil, insanity, and violence. I hoped these paintings could be upsetting, touching, funny: in short, I wanted to make works that could elicit strong feeling, although I knew it was an uphill battle: artworks don't tend to cause the same emotional reactions as books and movies do, maybe because their obvious artifice—their "object-ness"—gets in the way of storytelling. It's harder to get swept up in a still image, harder to suspend disbelief. The truth is, people are rarely brought to tears by paintings.

Around ten in the morning, I set out walking the mile from my garden apartment to my studio in the Brooklyn Navy Yard, my beloved dog, Jojo, in tow. It was early June but already over ninety degrees. The extreme heat was accompanied by humidity and a dirty gray sky, and the typically energetic Jojo was sluggish, her face pulled into a panting pit bull smile. The streets were empty for a weekend morning, and the premature heat had rendered my neighborhood and its denizens slightly foreign, almost eerie. Likewise, passersby seemed to regard me with an especial curiosity. I wondered briefly if it was my sweating that caused these sidelong glances—I'm convinced I sweat inordinately for a skinny woman—but discounted the idea quickly; given the climate, dry skin would be the creepy exception today.

The Brooklyn Navy Yard was first active at the beginning of the nineteenth century. During World War II, it employed as many as 70,000 people, at which time it was also the site of a naval prison, which was later converted to a regular prison, before being destroyed in

2005. Today it spans about four square miles, a winding network of streets and old factory lofts, and is zoned for industrial usage, housing businesses and artist studios. Enclosed by towering brick walls and accessible only via three guarded gateways, the Navy Yard continued to evince a sense of secrecy and importance—a sense that always evaporated when my own faded ID card granted me entrance.

On this day, the Navy Yard was empty. As Jojo and I walked from the gateway toward my studio building, I noted that a false wall had been constructed on one of the adjacent streets, which appeared to be covered with Wild West–style wanted posters. Intrigued, I approached, and, turning the corner, saw that the whole street had been transformed into a corny facsimile of a cowboy town. Shoddily constructed buildings comprised the old-timey commercial strip—with signs identifying the differently colored stores as Saloon, General Store, Haberdashery, Boot Shop, et al.

Ignoring my unease, I continued walking. Jojo, suddenly unaffected by the heat, began pulling on her lead and sniffing wildly, and I did my best to restrain her. It must have been for a movie, I thought, but a low-budget one. Everything looked structurally flimsy, as well as unconvincing. The posters that had initially caught my attention were smattered on seemingly every surface. Whoever had made them hadn't bothered with variation; each was an identical, artificially yellowed 8½ by 11 with a sepia photo of a ruggedly handsome, mustachioed man, captioned:

WANTED, DEAD OR ALIVE:
PETE "PICKAXE" PINCUS
FOR BANK ROBBERY, MURDER

Still holding tight to Jojo's leash as she frantically pulled me toward one of the buildings, I wondered whether Pickaxe was the film's protagonist or villain. We reached the storefront in question, identified by sign as the haberdashery, and Jojo's frenzy increased; I issued some half-hearted words of calm, but she continued to jump, bark, and whimper at the storefront. The glass was covered in an opaque layer of dirt, preventing me from seeing inside, but I was suddenly aware of what must have been driving the dog so crazy: the thick odor of rot.

Against what now felt like better judgment, I pulled my shirtsleeve over my fist and wiped away a circle of filth from the window. Jojo, now quiet again, looked at me, her head tilted in concern, as I lowered my head and peered in, expecting to see a dead squirrel or raccoon, at worst a stray cat.

It took some ten seconds for my eyes to adjust to the dim light in the dust-covered interior, a square room with a shadowy mass smack in the middle. My body registered the sight before my mind could. My abdomen and stomach tightened violently, my vision blurred, my knees gave way. I could feel my body giving way, acquiescing to gravity, the pavement pulling me closer. Just before I hit the ground and lost consciousness, the picture finally hit my cortex: a man in a rumpled cowboy costume, tied with rope to a chair, his big white hat askew and a huge pickaxe lodged in his skull.

I awoke to Jojo licking my face and whining. I don't know how long I was out. My head throbbed from where it hit the ground. A momentary amnesia turned to shock, which gave way just long enough for me to squeeze my phone from my jeans pocket and dial 911.

The 911 operator asked me my emergency and, shivering in spite of the heat, I stammered that I'd found a body. Is he breathing, ma'am? No, or I don't know. He's not, I don't know. He's dead, I think, he looks dead.

She asked me my location and I began to describe the set, the storefronts, the dirt and dust.

Ma'am, can you tell me where you are? The cowboy street, on the right side. The shivering was growing more intense.

Ma'am? Can you give me a geographic location?

Oh, I said, and began to laugh. Ma'am? The Navy Yard. The Brooklyn Navy Yard. By the Clinton Street entrance.

I ended the call, and began laughing again. People react to trauma in surprising ways, I said, explaining myself to Jojo, who at this point had lain down by my side and was licking my free hand. The smell of rot, I noticed, was gone. I closed my eyes and waited for sirens.

I slipped back out of consciousness and woke up surrounded by EMTs and cops. Miss, a cop was saying, miss. Are you the one who called?

He's in there, I said, pointing at the building in front of me.

The cop walked over to the window and put his face up to the spot I had wiped clean, cupping his hands around his eyes. He was still for a few seconds. It's empty, he said. I watched him as he avoided my gaze, looking at his colleague. Just a lot of dust, it looks like.

I looked at the building again. There was no more sign on its facade, no cheesy wanted posters. The EMTs were chattering about getting me onto a stretcher.

I stood up and smiled at the closest EMT. I'm fine, OK? He was handsome, with drawn, roughly shaven cheeks and an anachronistic mustache. He smiled back. Yes, he said. OK. Ignoring the cops' shouts for me to stay put, I picked up Jojo's leash and began to walk toward my studio.

Jonas Kyle

GLTE

10:16 AM MONDAY, EST.

706 million texts transmit to unique phone numbers, across all carriers around the world, in the language correlated to the number. "Your sister is dead," "your father is dead," "your daughter is dead," "your mother is dead," "your son is dead," "Adam is dead," "Melissa is dead," "Yao Shao is dead," "Ichika is dead," "Dashwee is dead," "Tanya is dead," "your best friend is dead," "Tutu dead in fifteen," "Gonzalo dead in five," "your husband dead in ten," "you will be dead in twenty-five" ...

10:24 AM MONDAY, EST.
ABERDEEN, TEXAS. NICENE ANALYTICS.
Twenty-three people in the Comprehensive View Room very alert. On surround screens and their own monitors, they observe in real time the inception and progression of the Great Lethal Text Event. GLTE. The initial blast, 706 million texts going out in three seconds to unique phone numbers from a draped master server entraining thousands of subjugate distributors, stresses networks impactfully around the earth. Sudden stresses are a bother if local, more serious if regional, but because it was, and is, universal, the case is very severe—and an immediate cause for unusual alarm. As seconds become minutes, the twenty-three observers in the Comp Room see cell phone use everywhere spike past installed measurement spectrums and across all platforms—text, facebook, emails, DMs, and voice calls. Parts of the cellular network around the world go dark, meaning extreme overload and failure. All those receivers of the texts must be frantically responding to them to see if the subject of the text is still alive and not dead.

"Is this a hoax?" Kaylene, chief of Instagram statistics, says to the room. Cutting through her words crack cries of extreme distress. Someone's down. Here's Kaylene: "What's that noise? Who ... who is it? It's Cutter. His face is blue. Heart attack! Oh my god. Aaah! Dammit! Siddhartha's collapsed just next to me and Arjay too." People respond into action, performing CPR on the three victims and calling Emergency. The calls to Emergency do get through, thanks to Nicene Analytics having the best multiple-networked lines. Even so, all victims are soon dead, joined by five more in the next five minutes. When Emergency shows up, themselves short two medics who expired on the way over, twelve of the original team of twenty-three working for Nicene Analytics have passed. Kaylene is doing her best to keep the survivors calm—who knows who will be next?

10:33 AM MONDAY, EST.
WEST VILLAGE, NYC.
"I am not a fucking loser! Did I really resign—did I *really* resign? Dammit! I did. I resigned.

They put me on their fucking *shitty men* list. That's a very poisonous list, ladies, I just want to say that. To quote Blake, 'I was angry with my friend, I told my wrath, my wrath did end. I was angry with my foe, I told it not, my wrath did grow.' Why didn't you tell me if you thought I was abusing my position? I helped make so many of you; because of me you're national writers. That's a fact, by the way, you can't take that back like the way you once loved me. Oh my god, I have a beautiful mind! I went to Harvard, for chrissake, got my MA at Bard. You can't just throw me under the bus like this. I have read five thousand books! And good, difficult, hard ones. And brought five hundred more to life, as diverse as fuck, published, because of me."

"Hello, Caleb."

Caleb looks over from the tree he is hugging on Barrow Street in the West Village, a small lane where hardly anyone ever walks. He sees a woman. Why does she know my name? She's wearing a pale-mauve cotton dress under a muted roseate blazer with bright highlights and a small green hat. Her heels are three inch. Her white calf gloves stretch halfway to her elbows. Caleb can't recognize her. He is at a loss.

"Who are you?"

"My name is Maeve. I was walking by and I noticed you were in some trouble."

"Me? Well I'm not … OK, yeah, I'm in trouble."

"Where's your phone? In your pocket?"

"I don't have it. I smashed it a while ago."

"How come?"

"Because my wife texted me we were done."

"Hmm, well, there is a major emergency going on. If you had your phone you would know about it."

"Umm, what do you mean? You mean one of those Flash Flood Emergency alerts?"

"No. OK, Caleb, well, here's the thing. We are in the midst of a Great Lethal Text Event, or GLTE. One tenth of the human population is being culled at this moment. Unfortunately, you are part of that cull. You received, not that long ago, a text informing you of your imminent demise. You have"—and Maeve looks at her wristwatch—"eight minutes to live."

"What!? Are you crazy?"

"Calm down, Caleb. Calm down. Relax and listen."

Caleb cocks his ears and hears very disturbing noise, most of it emanating from the east, over by 7th Avenue, and not as much, but still a lot, coming over from Hudson Street. A terrible saturation of emergency sirens, audible crashings of vehicles, thousands of people shouting, screaming. An explosion. It sounds like all hell is breaking loose on both sides. Caleb stares at Maeve, who is calmly standing near him, and gets the creeps.

"Are you here to kill me? Are you my assassin?"

"No, I am not. I am not a death angel. I am a wandering witness. Come over here, Caleb, sit down. Sit down beside me here on these steps."

Maeve has taken a seat four steps up on a brownstone stoop. She looks acutely beautiful, both to Caleb and just as she is. He complies. She puts her arm around his shoulder tenderly.

"Well, next time, honey, OK? Sorry this didn't work out."

"Am I really going to die, like right now?"

"I'm not sure. As I told you, I am just a witness. But your time, actually, it's up."

Caleb feels his chest tighten, huge shudders of volts go through him, he can't see and starts to fall back.

Ian Bosak

Legend of the Shooting Star

The question isn't how, *baby*, it's when. When (did you do that), that thing, you know *exactly* what I'm talking about. Bringing home a brand-new copy of Willmaster 5000 for Windows 98 PC, hearing the CD-ROM fucking whirrrr baby, take a look under the hood *baby*, this is some serious RAM ...

I don't miss him that way, I miss a notion
of him, maybe the part where he made them run screaming
through the halls announcing the death throes of a little day-
time-television delusion.

We all love a lil' fever dream now and then *baby*, a little drug relapse into that ole film spool of Mr. Owl Daddy use-ta play for us. What will you find when you find it? When you dig for it, how many times are you going to square off them sides and call it six feet deep, was it orange or red? (The Tootsie Pop [I hope it was orange].) But I told you *baby*, I'll be the scales of fucking justice for ya, I'll show you Nirvana, Unplugged at the fuckin Arby's on 132. We're going for broke on a Cheddar Beef Classic, and that sauce is gonna DR////////////P.

But first you gotta ask yourself, is it ripe? Is it that fucking ripe that you can't wait to cut that sucker open and forget the licks?

Good	Bad
Orange	Red (if unripe)

[The same applies to Gatorade (the ripeness of a red Gatorade should also be factored into this).]

It's OK *baby*, take the back seat we're riding shotgun with deliverance tucked down the side of our 34x30 Dickies sucking smoke through that eerie shade of blue that blows into the room on a December morning. We're gonna fucking blow this joint away, *baby*, you got Betty Sue and the Reaper wants Taquitos so we're going in skeeeeeerrr-eaaming *baby*, we're gone get those fuckin' pops and we're gonna be suckin' on gold, just you wait, you don't have to worry about a thing *baby*. You're gonna forget all about the kerning on that god-awful courier font, your sister's just gonna take the Xbox to the pawn shop anyways *baby*. I told you I went to the Smithsonian, I learned how to do this right, *baby*, I'm a scholar, I'm a fuckin' learn-ed man, I'm a got'dam American hero. We're gonna live forever and you're gonna frisbee that got'dam Willmaster disc right out the window and straight to the moon (earth's) *baby*, we got more brass than Sputnik and we're going places, we're three licks away from a got'dam *Chevy, baby*.

> *We were in the bedsheets slipping around like eels, it was all silk and*
> *prenatal vitamins, you always cared so much about those locks, we were a got'dam*
> *Robert Wiles photograph, it was tragic. Sprawled across a*
>   *Pillowtop slab, expressions (null) tasteful in their stalactites of drool.*
> *I couldn't tell if you were dead or just a beautiful*
> *wet element to catch the moonlight (? [is it a night scenario?])*

Alright *baby*, you know the plan, fuck the hot fries and the King Size Cups (to be read as Reese's [Normal, not the Big Cups, nor the Big Cups with Reese's Pieces], not Butterfinger), you know the plan? There's 7.6 billion got'dam people on this planet, so someone's gotta feel like us, we ain't ever gone get this chance again *baby*, I gotta know you're ready to RUMBLE. Pull that skull mask down ove—I don't give a fuck about your got'dam hair *baby,* no—you know what I mean, we got a got'dam stick-up to do right now *baby* this ain't the time! Now Remember, we gotta get them orange ones, you know the good stuff, but we gotta get the ones with them Stars, thems the ones that get ya a whole got'dam bag for free. Yes it's true, Mr. Owl ain't gone lie to the got'dam people—get your fuckin' mask on.

Now listen, you know what you gotta do, alls ya gotta do is call into the precinct and you tell him, "I know who killed the Boy In The Box, I know who he is, I'm lookin' right at em and he's waving a 45 Peacemaker around screamin' 'I'm a cowboy now ma! I'm a real-life cowboy!'" You got it? You gotta sound convincin' and I'll be down the road screamin' real hick-like and they'll come runnin'. That's when we get the hell out of dodge and down to the Chevron and Johnny Law'll be all wrapped up in that cold case, it'll be smooth sailin' *baby*. Alright Greyskull, you ready?

   It felt like a fugue state, the lilac peelin' off my finger-nails, I couldn't speak, I saw the bat crack, I was chokin' on my tongue, I couldn't scream, all of a sudden I remember you askin'
   for that Margarita recipe, damn fuckin' fool. There was a cockroach runnin'
            down your neck, it was beautiful baby, you looked
like a got'dam angel of death you shoulda seen the blood,

how it ran like ribbons in your hair.

It's all sugar 'n' smoke *baby*, just flash em the gun and get the gear, in and out while the po-lice are all wrapped up in that ghost we ouija'd out the grave. Stop sweatin' *baby* we's fine keep your head on a got'dam swivel, they ain't gone get us we made a pact with the got'dam Holy Ghost back in '67 Jesus himself gone put a hand to them slugs. Just stick to the plan.

\\\\\\\\\\ *It's like he was fuckin' waitin' for us.*

At that moment, Mr. Owl looked down over the Chevron, with a soggy stick leaning out of his beak, he chuckled. Looks like them boys got wrapped up, he said with a hoot. He could see one throw a fire extinguisher through the door, somethin' beat and bloody in his arms, it looked like roadkill.

Steam creeped out from the shower pissing down on a cheap plastic tub. The wavering, sometimes ghostly voices of the Carter Family Band haunting my fucking lungs like a slug that just won't shake the stick. We had a plan baby we were gone be rich, we were gone be fuckin' silver plated. I could feel Chet Atkins staring blankly into my eyes. We were gone make it baby. I grabbed my IMAX glasses from the dresser and put them over his eyes, nothin' but the best for my baby Chet, you gone be seein' them pearly gates in 1080p.

(There was a bit of a glint in Chet's glasses as the sound of a CD-ROM filled the Motel 6, it smelled like hot blood and steel, he looked at Chet one last time, and tucked the razor into an Orange Tootsie Pop wrapper.)

"Always knew you liked red better after all baby, always told you we was gone make a name for us baby, we was gone be legends, and they was gone see us shootin' the got'dam stars outta the sky."

Bob Nickas

Let's Play Live— From A to B and Back Again

A: What really haunts you?
B: Besides the people I cared about who we now call dead?

A: Besides them.
B: Two of whom we have in common.

A: Yes. But you don't believe in ghosts.
B: I don't. I believe in the memory of those who were once alive, their persistence, as they live on in our heads, for better or worse. I'm a ghost writer, you might say, but for myself. Scary fiction … that's never been for

me. I haven't once, for example, read a book by Stephen King. What can spiral violently out of control in the everyday, that's what horrifies me.

A: We're both more interested in true crime.
B: Lately I've been haunted by that fifteen-year-old boy who stabbed his teacher to death in the classroom, in front of all those terrified students, some of whom he had told he would do it, but they either didn't believe him or were afraid to say anything.

A: This was three years ago, in the UK.
B: This blessed plot, this scepter'd isle, this realm ... Lady Brexit, Little England more likely.

A: You're not an Anglophile.
B: Not on either side of the road. Though I'm not an Anglophobe. What we should all fear is small-mindedness, and small-mindedness looms larger than ever, on both sides of the Atlantic, and is fast becoming an epidemic worldwide.

A: That kind of murderous violence is uncommon there, which is why it was so shocking.
B: For a country that gave us Jack the Ripper, the Moors murderers, Ian Brady and Myra Hindley, and more recently the terror tweens Robert Thompson and Jon Venables, ten year olds who snatched two-year-old James Bulger off the street, tortured and killed him,

brutal, sadistic homicide is certainly a shock to the system. So rarely encountered.

A: The crime was also shocking because of the age of the killer.
B: Will Cornick, an intelligent boy with perfect attendance in school.

A: It had been twenty years since a teacher was murdered by a student in England.
B: This was in Leeds. Live at Leeds. At Corpus Christi Catholic College.

A: *Corpus Christi* … body of Christ.
B: Did you see his Facebook page?

A: He's wearing an *Achievement Hunter* T-shirt, and he has long hair, much longer than in his arrest photo.
B: There's a drawing of a grim reaper on his Facebook page, and under *Interests* it only says: women.

A: The women he was murderously interested in were his instructors.
B: Ann Maguire, his Spanish teacher, most of all. Writing to a friend on Facebook he said she "deserves more than death, more than pain and more than anything that we can understand."

A: I guess that friend didn't turn him in.

B: He also targeted a faculty member who was pregnant, wanting to murder her and, as he said, "to kill her unborn child."

A: Is it true that he asked one of his classmates to film the attack?
B: Oh yes, because unless a crime is filmed it's almost as if it hadn't happened. Once recorded and posted, the murder and his fame would live on. But it wasn't filmed.

A: He threatened to kill the boy he tried to enlist, as well as another he had spoken to beforehand.
B: Some students had seen the knife he brought to school that day.

A: Was it up the sleeve of his shirt?
B: Yes. And none who saw it reported him either. They didn't believe he would go through with it. I read that the boy was known for his dark sense of humor, so they didn't take him seriously.

A: Don't fear the reaper.
B: Actually there was a student who reported him, but this occurred just moments before, or even as the attack was happening.

A: Too late for him to be stopped.
B: Besides the knife, he had taken a bottle of whiskey to school.

A: He planned to celebrate after the murder.

B: You know what else haunts me? Right before he stabbed his teacher ...

A: From behind, in the neck and in the back.

B: He winked at one of the students in the classroom.

A: And as he was stabbing her, he was expressionless.

B: What else would he be? Wild-eyed?

A: His remarks to the psychiatrists who examined him are chilling. He said that after he had done it, "I wasn't in shock, I was happy. I had a sense of pride. I still do."

B: Absolutely no remorse. And even worse, proud of what he had done.

A: Achievement Hunter.

B: Cavalier ... carefree ... devil-may-care. When one psychiatrist asked how the murder would affect his teacher's family and friends, he said, "I couldn't give a shit. I know the victim's family will be upset but I don't care. In my eyes, everything I've done is fine and dandy."

A: Fine and dandy. So neat and tidy, so very British.

B: He also claimed that he didn't have a choice in the matter. "It's kill or be killed. It was kill her or suicide."

A: He should have taken his own life.

B: Well, his life is over, for all intents and purposes. He was sentenced to a minimum of twenty years in prison, at which time he'll be thirty-six. And yet it's hard to believe that he's going to be released. Although advocates for child criminals insist that their brains aren't fully developed, and rather than be given long sentences, a program of counseling toward rehabilitation is more appropriate, how can they possibly conclude that a fifteen year old doesn't know right from wrong in relation to taking another life. It's not all make-believe. It's not child's play.

A: Look at the case of those twelve-year-old girls who were infatuated with Slender Man …
B: In love with a fictional character they supposedly believed to be real.

A: They lured one of their classmates into the woods— to play hide-and-seek—then stabbed her nineteen times with a kitchen knife.
B: Every house has them.

A: They did this to impress Slender Man.
B: Nineteen times, but she somehow survived.

A: Did you see in the news that the girl who did the stabbing, Anissa Weier, who had pled insanity, was sentenced to twenty-five years in a mental institution? Then there's another three years of hospitalization after that, for good measure.

B: That girl is going to be thirty-seven when and if she finally gets out.

A: Almost the same age as Will Cornick. Maybe they can be jailhouse pen pals, and one day ...
B: Being placed in a mental institution may be worse than going to prison, because in a hospital setting you can actually be kept indefinitely, beyond the length of the sentence. I guess it's like being denied parole over and over again, although doctors are thought to have greater weight in their recommendations than a parole board.

A: Cornick said, "I wanted to get caught. That's why I did it in school. I wanted to be in jail." He didn't plead insanity. That might have required remorse.
B: I wonder if he ever read *Lord of the Flies*, a classic cautionary tale by a British author, William Golding.

A: Savagery lies beneath civility, dormant but all too easily aroused, especially in times of war.
B: The boy was not only proud of what he had done, he actually defended himself and rationalized an irrational act when he admitted, "I know it's uncivilized but I know it's incredibly instinctual and human. Past generations of life, killing is a route of survival."

A: And how was he, like that mob of schoolboys in *Lord of the Flies*, as they chased a squealing wild boar through the jungle, able to see his teacher as something to be slaughtered, as beneath him?

B: He told one psychiatrist that he thought of her as "barely human."

A: His favorite song, apparently, was "Jungle Boogie." He had played it at school on numerous occasions. He knew it from the movie *Pulp Fiction*.

B: In the end the most haunting aspect of this story is what he had to say, aloud to the other students in the classroom, after he stabbed the teacher. He calmly sat back down at his desk and with a sense of satisfaction said, *"Good times."*

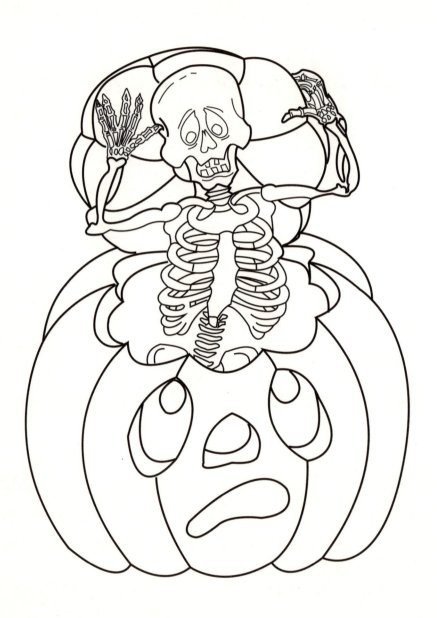

Riley Hanson

It's Cold in Here Bradbaby, and We're Going to Die

pressing lips
took many shapes
colored vibrant
from tears
with wild nights

I've never danced
I've never worn a gown
I want to dance all night
a woman in the spring
we must dance
oh please

—

my mouth twitched twice
it sighed and wept
being drunk could not drink

I called softly
where are you tonight?

the cat came first
she elongated her throat
looking from shadows
that funnel the wind
proclaiming
in a further layer
of darkness
it was not normal
for me to want
to be her

coffins
under bridges?

—

Ray Bradbury visited me at a bookstore I recently started
working at. I was holding a book for a customer while they
explained something about their son. It was as if I had some-
how read the book already or by holding it I understood

everything inside. As I held the book, I noticed that the corner was wet. I opened the book and the liquid began to spread on every page. I shook the book around, freaking out, and realized that it was starting to smoke. It then began to burn in my hands. Everyone around me noticed something was on fire and started yelling to put it out. I sort of smashed it in my hands in an attempt to stop the burning. The book burned, but as it burned it vanished into nothing and after the fire was out the book was gone. Everyone who was there was confused why I lit the book on fire but I desperately tried to explain that the ghost of Ray Bradbury had lit it on fire to fuck with me.

—

It's not me
underneath my front
are marks
from which I was
a piece
of paper
with writing
that said
your joy

—

everything can not be tormented
the way you want it to be
and there I lay with eyes beside me

a cat with claws instead of arrows
my heart was too deep in my chest

—

I rearranged my hands
in the bathroom
of a train with a limber floor
night was nine times longer
than the day before

the sheriff took his feet down
not a doctor
may I kiss you goodbye?
of darkness
illuminated only by
cannot explain

—

and after midnight
only wings
can drop wingless
and the wolf lies content
with the head of a goose
and I an old woman
from the grave
inhaling the man
solid flesh

—

I crawl back to the forest in
rabbit skin
to shuffle between the trees
near the creek

I dance
to be seen by a fox
how soon
I lay motionless
looking inward
feeling caught again
as the man with wings
stares across the aisle

—

*Ray Bradbury's ghost visited me in a library. Underneath it all
I knew he had collected different bullet holes from gunshots. He
wasn't crawling or anything, just standing there with his arms
hanging and his face silent. He was aging, and he was dead, even
though he said he would live forever. He called to me, standing
in four inches of water. I was in the sand but afraid to get closer.*

—

Ray was a farmer's wife
on the porch with a cradle

inside bones
cool in the painted fog
still unentertained
the sun goes down
I become frail
on four legs purring
lightly into a wind
beating moonlight
into a tight ball
that I paw at
until morning
I am burned into
soft ash in a fire
from hell

—

on the train there
Ray fell asleep in the aisle
I was a girl
with her mother
lips moist
clutching a crucifix
and the skies
suffering of
farewell winter
I was sent to write
dreams on his
waving hands

the people on this train
are killing you
they stared
and jumped
through his veins

—

his words moved
to tell me
who I am
upside down
the dining room
looked empty
I swallowed
in one silent
careful
someone write this down
the bells
flew back
blushing
I sang
in a frenzy
of blood
into screams

—

at a café
I strangle
a vast world
with my tongue
and tiny spikes
I hide back
in the womb
across the floor
a man shouted
he's behind your eyes
piercing through
the shrouded figures
enjoying love

will you look into my face and remember where you last
saw me?

—

*Ray Bradbury visited me as weed last night. Once he took
hold of my lungs I couldn't remember anyone's name. I wandered through a vacant house wondering if he would appear
on the rounding of a dark corner. I went home and lay on the
couch staring at the ceiling until he left.*

—

will you sharpen stakes?
be struck by lightning?

I leaned forward
from a nurse's lips
for another kiss
do I touch
and break through the cobwebs?
rare childlike ghosts
faded like sudden dreams
distant blaze
burning from the window
in my eyes
I don't want to move
I'm tired

—

Ray didn't come to the show I went to last night. I waited outside on the step next to the entrance smoking cigarettes and drinking wine. I checked my phone every thirty seconds to see if he would call from some random number, breathing deeply into the phone or something like that. The show ended and I followed the crowd to a bar down the street where the after-party was. I sat in a booth alone with my head tilted back, fluttering my eyes in my head to see if I could contact him. He didn't answer and I went home and went to sleep. He didn't even visit in my dreams. I woke feeling numb and uninteresting.

—

oh please we must dance
for five hundred years
you must hold my hands
we can cull new bodies
and be six in the graveyard
growing between
hysteria and celebration
can't you kill me now?
on my back
lapping milk
scratching promise in the sky

—

After a few days Ray visited and forced me to kill my family dog. It was brutal and I woke crying, wondering why he could be so mean. I went to New York that weekend, upset with Ray and the ways he was choosing to haunt me. Ray visited me that night at the bar for the last time. He was sweet, sitting in three seats at the same time. He quickly vanished into laughing and I went home wondering who else he was haunting.

Tommy Pico

Trap

I wake up. My right forearm. Up to the elbow. Is gone. Bloody gauze. My head. Is a fog. His voice rolls in.

"Delicious. Enlightening." He smacks. His lips. "Utterly relatable."

The swirling. Panic. Sets in again. Mouth too dry. To scream. How long? A day? Five days? Hope fluttered out. The fake. Window in hours. This is the apartment. I fell asleep in. His apartment. Last night. Nights ago.

"Please," I croak.

"Do you know where the word *trap* comes from?"

The darkness. Pulses. Falling again. Drag. Of the tide.

—

The way Leo's teeth fit together in his mouth, the top and the bottom meet like puzzle pieces. *I'll bet he's a grinder*, was Danny's first thought when they met. "I'm so stoked you came to the bar tonight," Leo waves at the country-western-themed, lacquered-wood beer and shot joint around them. "I mean you're a famous writer and I'm, like, a stranger from Twitter," Leo takes a sip of his Tecate and shrugs.

"Oh stop. Famous, my dude? Yeah right. There are like five poetry fags on the planet who know who I am, you just happen to be one of them," Danny smirks. Leo chuckles and looks down, before looking back up at Danny, giving an "aw, shucks" face. The sparklers in his eyes ripple and sway. "Plus we've followed each other for like a year now. Hardly a stranger in my book."

"You've been on tour for what, like six months now? You must be exhausted." Leo's nails are chipped salmon, tapping on the tabletop.

"It's a tour," Danny does air quotes as he says *tour*. "But that presumes it will end."

"What do you mean?" Leo leans in closer. When he first saw Leo in the doorway of the bookstore earlier that night, Danny had a Wayne-seeing-Cassandra-for-the-first-time moment. *Oh Dreamweaver.* It helped that Leo was wearing a tight black *Wayne's World* T-shirt, tucked into a pair of high-waisted, acid wash jeans.

"When the book dropped lo those months ago, I moved out of my apartment, put all my stuff in storage, and got on the Greyhound." Danny shakes his head and looks past Leo at the window. Outside, a drunk straight couple leaned into each other like cigarettes. "The idea of being in any one place for too long just felt ... suffocating. Everything felt like needing to open a window. I don't know, maybe this is just the way things are now." Danny takes a big gulp of his amber pint.

"That's so rad! I'm jealous." Leo leans back in his seat. "I've been in Seattle ... whew. Way longer than I ever wanted to be. I thought maybe a couple years after undergrad I'd move on to New York or something, but," Leo starts chewing on his nails. "Sometimes you get into a routine and suddenly it's six years later and you're still working at the same damn coffee shop."

Danny pauses for a few seconds before suddenly animating. "What should I see while I'm here? Not like dumb touristy Ferris wheel shit. What's like some real Seattle shit?"

"How long do you plan on sticking around?"

"The plan is to not have a plan."

Leo pauses, lost in thought for a minute, before coming back to himself. "Let's get out of here."

—

I creep. Awake.

"The old Dutch. It means *staircase*. It came to invoke the outline of a staircase, the step by step. The trap is the ensnarement, but also the descent. The lure ..."

My tongue. Gone. Bottom jaw. Gone. Three fingers on. My left hand. Left foot. I don't see. Speakers anywhere. It's like. He talks directly. Into my head.

"Mmm ... Dizzying. Neurotic. Exciting. I'm going to savor you for days." Grinding teeth. Fingernails snapped. Shudder on the. Sharp carpet. Gray spiders pluck. Pluck. Pluck. Across the ceiling.

Why. I try again.

"Exhilarating."

—

It's barely a park, just a patch of grass and a bench covered in graffiti, half-drank Rainier tall cans and empty packs of Camel blues.

"This is your favorite spot?" Danny looks confused.

"Don't look at the ground, look at the sky." Leo turns him around to face the sapphire Seattle skyline. The planes round down into Sea-Tac airport like string lights. Elliot Bay reflects the city in little, luminous spoonfuls. Leo pulls a flask from his jacket and tosses it at Tommy. "I've got some whiskey and this here *jazz cigarette*." Leo's cadence turns into mud as he lifts a joint out of his pocket. He brushes some of the refuse off the bench.

"Kick!" Danny sits next to Leo and takes the joint. They pass it back and forth a couple times, looking into Seattle. Leo clears his throat.

"I loved your book, I just have to say. I couldn't stop reading. It was so … stuffed, you know? So full of the world that it became rarefied. It really helped me when I—"

"Can you do me a favor?" Danny exhales into the summer skyline. "No offense, but the idea of people reading my work," Danny makes air quotes when he says *work*, "is kind of mortifying. Like, my skin started to crawl a little." He hands the joint back to Leo.

"I'm sorry, I just think you put something out into the world that is praiseworthy. I just wanted to give it some shine, that's all." Leo puts his hands up like surrendering.

"I know, it's not you." Danny knocks back some of the whiskey. "I want to get there, to be able to sit still and know my work is out there. To stay put."

Leo reaches his arm around Danny's shoulders. "I wasn't lying, what I said before. I would love to just be out on the road. I'm stuck here and spinning but at least you're out there spinning toward something."

"Am I? I can't tell anymore."

They sit in silence for a few minutes, at first looking toward the skyscrapers and the dark before slowly drawing their faces toward each other. They kiss in long shudders, stirring like a choppy sea. After a while Leo pulls away.

"Come back to my place?"

Danny nods.

"I mean like, you can chill here awhile if you want? You can just stay put. Like a few days or?"

Danny looks up at the sky, exhaling loudly, before returning his face to Leo's. "Yeah, OK."

—

I. Am. Up. Alive. I. Am. To. Alive. I. Am. The. Alive. I. Am. Knee. Alive. I. Am. Left. Alive. I. Am. Alive. Arm. Shoulder. I. Am. Alive. Left. I. Ear. Am. Alive. Can't. I. Am. Reach. Alive. I. Out. Am. Alive. I. Move. Am. Alive. I. Am. Right. Alive. Shoulder. I. Am. Alive. I. Am. Alive. I. Am. Alive.

"There really isn't that much of you left is there? Oh really, this has been one of the best. Redolent of galloping horses."

Grinding. I. No. Am. Water. Alive. For. I. Tears. Am. This. Alive. Is. I. The. Am. Last. Alive. I. Time. Am. Isn't. Alive. It.

"Once more, for old time's sake, ha, ha, ha. OK. *You are getting very sleepy.*"

—

Danny wakes up in Leo's apartment, shaking off the boozy haze, with Leo's arms wrapped tightly around him. *Jesus,* he thinks, wriggling from Leo's grip slowly before gathering his things in careful quiet. *Not feasible, my dude.* Danny writes a thank you note, tucks it under the pillow, before turning down the unusually long hallway toward the front door. As he turns the knob, Danny clocks that the door is locked but the knob is smooth. The door is locked from the other side.

Danny turns and walks back toward the bedroom, thinking maybe there's an automatic lock situation. Maybe a buzzer? He was hoping to avoid telling Leo he wasn't staying but now it couldn't be avoided. To his surprise, Leo is no longer in the bed. And the blanket is smoothly draped on his side as if it hadn't just been slept in. Danny checks the kitchen, the small closet, and the bathroom. The only other rooms in the apartment. Nothing.

"Leo?" Danny feels a slight twinge of panic before talking himself down. There is literally nowhere for Leo to go. He must be here somewhere. Danny walks to the window and opens the curtains thinking even though they're a few flights up maybe there's a fire escape or something. But it's not a window behind the curtains. It's a light box.

"What the fuck?" Danny backs up, looks around the room, looks up, looks down the hall, now feeling a full surge of electricity. He raps on the light box. Knocks on it. Pounds. "Fuck this." Danny grabs a tall, thin end table next to him, readies a swing, and pummels it against the light, smashing it to pieces but thrusting the room into darkness. Tinkling glass echoes against the floor.

Danny fumbles around the room for a light switch and flips on the power. Behind the shattered light box it's solid concrete. Danny walks up to it, knocking more glass away, and pounds on the wall. He looks around the room for something solid and spies a table lamp. He rushes through the hallway to the door, strikes the handle. Over and over. Screaming. Until it breaks off. Danny throws the lamp to the ground and flings open the door. The same concrete. Screaming. Hands on head. Running back to the bedroom.

"Leo! Please Leo this isn't cool, what's going on?!?"

A voice sounds. As if right into his head. "Calm down." Danny looks around. To see where it's coming from. The voice is flat, a plain, not coming. From any direction. Everywhere and nowhere.

"Leo, what the fuck dude let me the fuck out!"

"You're not going anywhere. Isn't this what you wanted? To stay put?"

"I'm ... please, just—"

"You are going to start feeling droopy. Let yourself pool. I'm not a sadist, I won't do it when you're awake for god's sake."

The grinding sound. The lip smack.

"It's time to break fast."

Zach Smith

Beavis & Butthead Go to PS1

We're on our way to see Genesis P-Orridge perform or whatever. The GPS lady says we're five minutes away from PS1. I look over at Butthead and he turns to me, taking his eyes completely off the road. His neck veins twitch with each outraged horn honk from the confused dumbasses swerving around us. Butthead's neck looks like his cock.

We come up to our exit and jarringly switch four lanes as Sabbath blares from the Zune I bought Butthead for our anniversary. I remember the day Butthead lost his shit and threw a Lars Ulrich signature series drum stick at me from across our squalorous living room, screaming I had cheated on him. But to be quite honest Butthead just isn't enough for me sometimes. I'd be lying if I said I didn't regularly wrap a belt around my neck and climax dangling in our closet. It is in these moments of meditation that my visions of our life together reach their full potential.

Butthead parallel parks like thirteen inches from the curb a few blocks south of PS1. He just slapped me. I forget why. His eyes focus on the Long Island City thoroughfare. I'm trying to process whether or not we should cross the street. I'll let Butthead make the call. I wonder after all these years how he thinks though, if he even does at all. Definitely a lot of lizard brain tumbling around in that mongoloid cranium. I space out staring at his face and forget where I am. His profile makes me think of several butt-cracks prolapsing at once.

As you already know, I'm sure, the two of us are very frugal. We skip the museum front office, half hidden behind the erected concrete wall that clashes with the whole "get it, we used to be a school" facade. At the nondescript brick side we hoist each other through an open window. This puts us in the new Daria Morgendorffer retrospective, and you know I gotta say it's pretty good. And you know there's something else I wanna say. I scored with Quinn Morgendorffer. Definitely don't ask Butthead because it's true.

We find the right room, take our seats and wait for Genesis to emerge from wherever. It's filled with hot twentysomethings uniformly blessed with perfect cheekbones. Some of their mid-thigh-length lightweight coats are vintage, while others are $$$$. I have to restrain myself from pulling my Metallica tee over my head. I still might spaz out and rip my clothes off, who knows.

"Alright let's have a look," a British accent cuts through the room, quiet already but for a few nasal voices mumbling unintelligibly. With nary a short pause, the young patrons raise their hands. And behold, a wide variety of what I could only call boners, sort of, lit by cell phone LCD displays. "Phones off," notes Genesis. The cocks drip bioluminescent ooze. Oh I should preface this by saying: I'm not sure what year it is for you, but here it's 2017. Body mods are everywhere and 4D printed phalluses are passé. We've seen it and we get it.

The ceiling's white glass tubes go up, courtesy of Klaus Biesenbach in the corner fading the wall switch to mood lighting. Orange contrasting hues touch on the crowd's regally gaunt cheekbones. They hold inquisitively raised eyebrows bent to strained insouciance. All together they must be mind-melding to solve the world's aesthetic dilemmas. I half expect a makeup artist to come in and rosy all their cheeks with blush. And now Genesis reveals herself. She's been standing on a chair in the center of the room all along. She speaks: "I need all of you to situate yourselves in the shape of the mark of Eldritch Eros from the pamphlets you took in the lobby where you signed your waivers." Butthead and I had missed that part. Genesis continues, "Together we will now experience an elevated state of gender reversal: role inversion." She gives a nod and flashes Klaus a deformed gang sign. Klaus steps out into the hall and drags back in a 4D scanner. He sheepishly waves and dips out almost gracefully, but for a stray earbud dangling from his khakis, that he trips over. I turn away and fall into eye contact with Genesis, who has the facial expression of a poor soul whose head is about to be burst by a scanner but somehow enjoys it. Her pupils dilate to deep unnatural voids. I can't handle this for long and check back in with Klaus.

Doing so, a surreal oversight in my initial close viewing of Klaus's inability to navigate physical spaces reveals itself. What I thought were tangled Apple cords turn out to be ropes of drying cum. Then I note there is, in fact, cum everywhere. Like walls bleeding in horror movies except cum. I feel a pang, an intuition, and choke back "I'm Cornholio" from escaping my throat. I do manage, "Butthead. Hey Butthead, maybe we should get outta here."

Genesis speaks again and breaks my concentration. "Now," she proceeds, "no one leaves this room till we shake hands, all of us. No two of you are alike, but all are

compatible. Let the Chaos Deity speak through you."
An otherworldly sexual tension permeates all circulat-
ing oxygen. I space out for half a second and suddenly
Genesis is hanging from the ceiling upside down prop-
ping herself up with phallic tentacles gouged through
her skin. Aside her, a long protuberance emerges from
the ceiling. Seemingly with a libidinous mind of its own,
it squirts fluid on the dazed art patrons' faces.

I breathe a wave of pure pleasure from the institu-
tionally sanctioned air. I blink and open my eyes to
every fantasy I've ever had, synthesized in one gesture, stretched before me like a permanent wound.
Somewhere a Dionysian godhead, most likely the dude
from Gwar, is smiling. So, now sexually barren, free of
earthly wants, I crave an abstract fullness—kind of like
a mix of nachos and every genital organ arrangement
ever to exist combined.

Memories layer, benign and pornographic. Multicolor
spiritual release ensues. Aeons-old life-producing caves
push out caul-drenched surrogates. Ideas grow into
bodies and proceed to mate with humans. They pig out
on orgone flesh grown in a secret occult lab Klaus keeps
hidden deep inside PS1. It's a miracle we all have room
to do our thing in this basically windowless walk-in
closet of an excuse for a lecture hall. Good looking out,
junior curatorial fellows.

Erotic special powers, like Adobe tool functions made manifest, run rampant. Another tentacle grows out of a wall. This one seems friendly and I feel like he and I would get along. New growths blur out of the art patrons. Sentient oddities twist through each other like slugs mating in Butthead's favorite YouTube video.

"This is pretty cool," I say and turn to him. We stare deeply for a long time at each other's eyeballs. I plunge our shared tentacle mutation deep into a stranger's blooming orifice. I sit back, just really kick back and recline trying to read Butthead using pheromones. Butthead sprouts singing hummingbird organs of delicate curiosity. He brings his distended breast up to eye level and my retinas gush hot-pink high-res lube.

Looking like a fawn with starved-out cheekbones, a lone waif coyly eye-fucks Butthead from across the room. The Fawnboi's clothes are fused to his emancipated body. He gorges himself on green slime and pus-white berries from who knows where. He appears both naked and baroquely overdressed; head to toe in alien bio-mech couture. He loves the onslaught of attention, the admiration of sentient pleasure centers reaching him from all across the Kinsey Scale. Rhythmic bursts of Skene's gland fluid hit his face. Bard MFAs line the walls awestruck, not quite initiated.

Butthead is basically circular breathing. I've never seen

him cum this much. Strange glowing liquids fly in all directions, crisscrossing in midair. A pink mist evaporates their foreign toxins into a new compound, hovering ambrosial blueberry notes over the orgy.

The art patrons edge closer and closer to melding. Few can still be identified as autonomous life forms. A complex growth of synapses moves to eradicate a single brain of origin. The multisentient horde redlines its growing pleasure bandwidth, edging close to maxing out and maybe dying together. Still though, subversion rears its head. A boring-looking couple has vanilla missionary in a corner, flanked by paper towels.

Butthead revs his laugh up at another minor faction: a scrum of art bros gnawing through each other's clothes, mixing crushed-up bits of Google Glass with DMT-rich brain matter. The Fawnboi watches us watching the spectacle. He orients his giant taut thin legs at a provocative angle to flex his considerable hip muscles at us. A mass of tendrils appears and then hides away again under a discrete flap of athleisure draped at his midsection. He lets out a multiphonic sigh and a scorpion tail grows powerfully from his back. Jointed like an index finger, it juts out and violently stabs an awaiting orifice on Butthead. Butthead's skin is now a network of openings and closings, a switchboard of primeval energy channeling birth, death, waste, and food. All exhibition programming to the contrary, PS1 has manifested a beatific state. Genesis stands on a chair in the corner, beaming with approval.

Butthead and I awake in our shared bed of many years, in the house where as feral teenagers we defeated poverty and fame. Every day convinces me we're going to break up. But until then I'll savor this towering dumbass presence in my life. We'll keep on keeping on—Ozzy and Sharon, Gilbert and George, Thelma and Louise. Sometimes I wrap a belt around my neck and picture Laurie Anderson squeezing Lou Reed's dying hand.

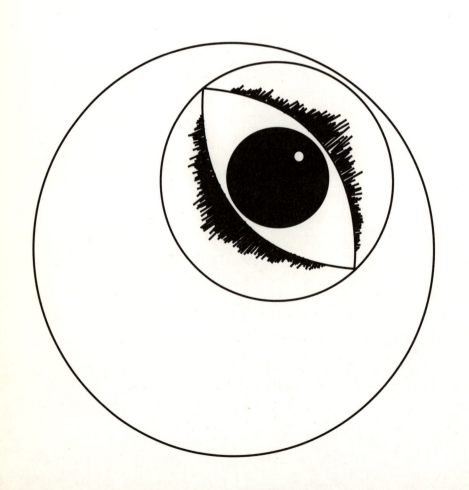

Amy Rose Spiegel

The Ooze

I am see-through black. I am not oleaginous but smooth, almost soft, like velvet. I am taking over the entirety. I will muffle the world.

The ooze crept from the inside of the moon, which, I learned later, had suddenly turned course then cracked open like an egg for breakfast on the perimeter between our atmosphere and the rest of everything's. In its terrible freedom, the ooze oozed down from the moon.

It was hard to notice the ooze at first, since space looks black to us, and when it reached an altitude where we might see it, it arrived at night for half of the planet. The other half, the daytime half that I was on, saw it as a hellish blanket, the covers being pulled up over the sun itself. When the ooze slunk all the way across the sun, a process which took from 5:54 a.m. to 9:21 p.m. EST, it had the prismatic effect of making it look like there were three suns in the sky. It was a reflection. Things got hot and dark.

I really saw it around nine, when the new suns were nearly all placed in their perfect awful column. I shook my boyfriend, Kyle, awake.

"Wake up. Wake up, something is really wrong with the sky. Oh, my gosh, oh fuck, Mary mother of God."

"Baby ..." Kyle was used to me mooning about the sky and otherwise freaking out, which had never pissed me off this bad before, which was really saying something special.

"Just LOOK. LOOK OUTSIDE."

"What are—fuck, what the fuck!" He repeated this in freakout staccato until I forced a glass of water on him to help him to stop. Unfortunately, it came out from the tap as though boiled for tea.

I like to take my time, as though drawing across a proscenium slowly for maximum dramatic effect before returning for good, to turn off the stage, a little later.

Kyle and I sewed our hands tight. We turned on New York One as though it were any other morning and we wanted to dunk on the anchors and policymakers we knew from waking up every day together. We caught a woman, grim in her lipstick, in the middle of saying that the mayor had something to say. Kyle took off his shirt; he was so hot. Mayor de Blasio, translucent with perspiration through his own shirtsleeves but apparently still feeling beholden to propriety despite the magnified weather, cleared his big-ass throat.

You had your priorities wrong.

"Our priorities right now," the mayor said, "are to work with this city's scientists and astronomers—the best in the world—to figure out how to keep New Yorkers safe. This unprecedented meteorological event ..." The tallest mayor started to cry. It wasn't clear if that was why the broadcast was cut.

"Kyle," I said. "The dream I had about you the other night. The one I said was nice but didn't want to describe how. You gave me a red marble and I knew it meant you wanted to get married, which I somehow loved the idea of. If we die, please let me do it first, whatever."

"We have to get the fuck out of here, or stay here until this passes, but we need time and like more information, baby."

I've always had ideas about what to use you for; yes I have my own version of a brain. Like yours. Throughout my system, like you in your body, I feel, consider, and know things, have always known you too. None of what I know is good for you. I can't wait to touch you.

"It's the SKY blacking out, Kyle. It's the freaking presumable PLANET. Can we please please get drunk, fuck each other, and tell each other times we have ever been happiest, and write all this down in case someone here survives." I believed in the good and preventative properties of history, his mine and everyone's, even though history had never given us what we needed to know what to do about this, to combat the ooze. I wanted to write down that ooze could come, in case it was helpful later on.

"Absolutely not are we doing that, Amy Rose. We need to block the windows and make a plan. I'm going to save your life."

"And yours?" (Anyway, mine was his.)

"You told me what you wanted, and we're going to be together, whatever it means." So I took his cue and painted the windows black, mimicking the ooze. Could we beat it at its own game?

"I didn't want to hurt you," but I knew I was going to and so I guess I did want to. I wanted what we had to last, and I wanted to hold all of you, too much, join you too much, glue us together, create something permanently dried in place, here we are, me contaminating and enveloping you.

In the air-conditioned multisun heat, my fake eyelash glue melted. I howled because the hot adhesive was leaking into my eyes, sealing them, and even though I wasn't sure I wanted to see what the ooze had planned for everybody next, it seemed cataclysmic to be sightless for whatever Kyle had to do from here on out to try and out-ooze it.

I didn't have to say "help me." Kyle, whom I thought must now have gotten naked—we joked that he always was—filled the bathtub with cold water and what ice cubes and frozen vegetable boxes he had in the refrigerator. We sat waist-deep and cross-legged as he set about with tweezers, plucking out my lashes until I could force my eyelids open, splashing my face with the icy water throughout to cool the glue for extraction. From the little blacked-out window above the shower we heard screaming and praying, were calm, did not want to do that yet.

I love you.

When I could see again, Kyle held up his tweezers hand. It looked wrong: dark with wetness from the inside, not just from the chilly water, and when I went to dry it, it smeared. The skin on his hand smeared. Blurred black like when there's too much ink, which began running down his forearm. I moved away from him.

How does it feel when I touch you now?

Kyle was still but didn't look dead but I couldn't touch him to see because I didn't want to stain more of him all over the bathtub. "Baby we are going to be OK," I said. "Baby just stay right where you are. I'm here."

I almost stopped moving when you did, but I wasn't done without you.

The street was quiet outside; no more screamers or prayers. Kyle, perfect and yes naked, didn't move. He was unresponsive. His face remained set in its determination to make us right again.

Remember I have always known you. I know you've always wanted to know me, too, and I always wanted to give you the chance.

I felt something crack open inside of me, like breaking

suddenly, like a forcible hatching. My feet were leaking and covering the bathroom tile in twinkling, rotten, thin tar. It was outer space, but on the floor. The ooze was soft, like velvet. It ruined everything.

If you touch me you can come with me and there is no other way.

Poison, inevitable, here I was at last. I stroked his cheek and cried.

Francesca Gavin

Hell Bound

Has anybody seen the devil? Mephistopheles has not got a clear-cut image anymore. The iconic personification of evil has disintegrated and become absorbed into all other aspects of modern life. Hell is no longer a metaphorical space. It is within the landscape and the architecture, within our own bodies, within communities, within technology. Hell is humanity itself.

In the current century there has been an increasing amount of artwork that plays with the imagery of horror, death, torture, and violence. A gothic blackness. Why now? The cliché that horror is an expression of millennial anxiety doesn't fit. The "fin de siècle" syndrome. The idea that as century or millennium approaches we panic about the end of the world, and this spills out into a culture of horror. The year 2000 has come and gone and the taste for the gothic is increasing. Nor does this explain the penchant for horror imagery in the 1940s, 1960s, 1980s. We are far enough into the twenty-first century for it to be founded on something else.

One argument is that the gothic is a response to what Michael Moore coined "the culture of fear" in his film on America and guns, *Bowling for Columbine*. He argues that teenage ultraviolence is partly a response to the contemporary media's sensationalist reportage of crime and violence. It could be claimed that horror in contemporary art is another step in this violent cycle. Shootings are created in response to a culture of materialism and fear. Art is created in response to the shootings. There's nothing new about that idea. The Marquis de Sade argues in his examination of the novel, *Idée sur les romans*, that gothic literature "was the inevitable result of the revolutionary shocks which all of Europe has suffered." He established the idea that the manifestation of horror in creativity was a response to a world desensitized to violence. While Baudelaire complained about the sensationalist aspect of the media in the 1860s, calling newspapers a "tissue of horrors" and an "orgy of universal atrocities."

Arguably the media has always been preoccupied with shocking imagery and violent narrative. "Being a spectator of calamities taking place in another country is a quintessential modern experience," as Susan Sontag put it in her book *Regarding the Pain of Others*. Positive news has always been in the minority (except when propaganda is in place). The media is a reflection of the ideology of everyday society. Slavoj Žižek observes in Alfonzo Cuarón's documentary *The Possibility of Hope*, that the main mode of politics today is fear—of immigration, of a strong state, of taxation. People in the modern world are mobilized through fear and pleasure.

So what are we so afraid of? Anything that transgresses the safe, cultural codes of "civilization." Anything that crosses between reality and fantasy, social laws and taboos, the rational and irrational. There is a lot to be afraid of these days. Exploring dark imagery or ideas in art arguably helps create a sense of control in a world where we have none. Catherine Spooner argues in the book *Contemporary Gothic* that the "gothic contains our fears so we can live in safety." That safety is looking pretty tenuous. This imagery reflects our struggle to have an identity in a society losing its sense of self.

Horror also connects to one of our most primal desires—voyeurism. The imagery of death and evil could be a metaphor for art itself—the uncontrollable desire to look. By looking at violence or horror we become complicit in its creation, part of the cause—hence part of the discomfort in looking. We know that humans are often the cause of terror, not some outside imaginary evil force. We are creating our own nightmares.

Contemporary gothic artworks are as much about the creation of art itself as the political or sociological zeitgeist. This is post–Pop art, which references imagery of daily life and the media, in order to connect to its audience. It was an approach pioneered by Andy Warhol's screen prints of the electric chair or car crashes. The gothic is a contemporary language that people can connect to on an instinctual level. The artworks that reference horror or the gothic are often not dark or negative. Horror is a language we can use to look at all the other issues in life. These images have been interpreted as Freudian, Marxist, feminist, semiotic, imperialist. The gothic can be whatever you want it to be.

It would be wrong to throw anyone who uses black paint into the same creative pigeonhole. The gothic as a reference is something that emerges at different periods in artists' works. That thread of dark imagery or ideas reflects very different aims and desires—and many different forms of expression. There are monsters, the grotesque, violated or mutant bodies, the divided self, ghosts, dolls, masks, skulls, disgust, and the abject. These are images filled with the color black, decay, and instability. Fear is reflected onto the environment, or onto the self, or onto others. Sometimes the work is nihilistic or anarchic.

Often expressions of horror are self-referential and poke fun at the genre's fairground imagery. Humor is central to so much of this artwork. Sometimes it verges on hysteria; sometimes self-conscious irony; sometimes it is a vehicle for political satire. Alex Da Corte's playful fluro neon-gothic references sit in this space. His darkness is rarely black. Instead it is a heavy, heady boudoir-like red. He references the suburban staged horror of haunted houses, the campiness of the Wicked Witch of the West, the cartoon-cultural clichés of the single barren tree, spider, or the pointed witch hat. These references are triggers for reactions in the viewer. They give his installations narrative strands that we all subconsciously know how to navigate, touching on our own childish nightmares and horror-attraction to space, darkness, and the monstrous. It is possible to see hints of the subtext of "the other" as a cultural bogeyman here. Da Corte unmasks and embraces these sexual and social outsiders. In his vibrant, pulsating landscapes, we want to be a part of their otherness.

Bret Easton Ellis's novel *Lunar Park* is a perfect expression of a wide-open, twenty-first-century horror. In this novel, the writer-protagonist is haunted by his own literary creations. Terror is projected onto the entire landscape—the house he lives in becomes a living, breathing creature of fear. Reality and fantasy blur. This is what makes contemporary horror so effective and intriguing. We question where art stops, and where real life begins.

A version of this text appears in the author's *Hell Bound: New Gothic Art*.

Contributors

Dan Allegretto is a well-known North Brooklyn layabout.

Al Bedell is a writer in Brooklyn.

Alissa Bennett is the author of *Dead Is Better*, a twice-yearly periodical that examines the seedy underbelly of popular culture. Her fiction has appeared in monographic publications for Bjarne Melgaard, Darja Bajagić, and Piotr Uklański.

Ian Bosak is a writer and sometimes artist residing in Philadelphia with notes of conifer, Werther's Originals, and diet tonic.

Tommy Brewer is an acclaimed small-business owner and fine-art enthusiast.

Charlie Fox is a writer who lives in London. His first book, *This Young Monster*, is out now.

Noel Freibert is the editor of *WEIRD Magazine* and creator of the graphic novel *Old Ground*.

Francesca Gavin is the author of six books, has a monthly radio show, Rough Version, on NTS.live, and has curated exhibitions at the Palais de Tokyo, MU Eindhoven, and co-curated the Historical Exhibition for Manifesta 11 in venues including Kunsthalle Zurich and Migros Museum.

Riley Hanson is an artist and writer living and working in Philadelphia, PA.

Jonas Kyle lives and works in New York City. He is cofounder and co-owner, with Miles Bellamy, of Spoonbill & Sugartown, Booksellers.

Sam McKinniss is an artist in New York.

Bob Nickas is the author of *The Dept. of Corrections*, *Painting Abstraction*, *Theft Is Vision*, and the forthcoming *Komp-laint Dept*. He is the proprietor of May 68.

George Pendle's books include *Strange Angel*, *Death: A Life*, and *Happy Failure*. He has scribbled for *Esquire*, *Frieze*, and *The Economist*, and scrawled catalogue essays for Carroll Dunham, Michael Williams, and Dan Colen.

Kaitlin Phillips lives on the Upper East Side. She writes for *Artforum*, *Bookforum*, and *n+1*.

Tommy Pico is a poet from the Viejas Indian Reservation of the Kumeyaay Nation. His Myers Briggs is IDGAF.

Sarah Nicole Prickett's writing has appeared in *T Magazine*, *The New Inquiry*, *Artforum*, *Interview*, and *n+1*. She is the editor and cofounder of the modern erotica journal Adult.

William Pym is a writer, teacher, and art dealer. From 2008 to 2009 he wrote "Bones' Beat," a pseudonymous weekly column about morality in the New York art world, for the *Village Voice*. He lives in Kent, England.

David Rimanelli is contributing editor at *Artforum*. His writing has appeared in publications including the *New Yorker, Bookforum, Interview, Frieze*, and the *New York Times*.

Collier Schorr was commissioned by Brendan Dugan to write about the remake of the *Ghostbusters* movie. It was a dare.

MT Shelves is the author of the comics *1-800-MICE, INFOMANIACS*, and *Art Comic*.

Jeremy Sigler is the author of books including *My Vibe, Crackpot Poet*, and *ABCDEFGHIJKLMNOPQRSTUV WXYZ*. He is the coeditor of *Carl Andre: Sculpture as Place, 1958–2010*.

Amy Rose Spiegel is a blonde Don Juan who wrote the nonfiction collection *Action: A Book About Sex*, published by Grand Central. Her other writing is in *Rolling Stone, The Guardian, NME, The FADER*, and plenty of other places.

Jia Tolentino is a staff writer for the *New Yorker* lol.

Published on the occasion
of the exhibition

Alex Da Corte
C–A–T Spells Murder

February 17–March 18, 2018

Karma
188 East 2nd Street
New York, NY 10009

Cover image: Bill Schmidt

Open Window
Director: Alex Da Corte
Producer: Ted Passon
    and David Dunn
Associate Producer:
    Shannon Sun-Higginson
Director of Photography:
    Zachary Rubino
Gaffer: Pauly D.
Makeup: Chi-Chi Saito
Wardrobe: Cara Yarmolowicz
3-D Animation/Compositing:
    Harvey Benschoter and
    Jared Defrees
Colorists: Amy DiLorenzo
    and Lenore Romas
Score: Zach Morgan
Frightened Girl #1:
    Annie Clark
Frightened Cat: Dylan the Cat

Thank you to all of the spooky
souls who contributed their words
and time to this book.

Thanks to the family and
Hudson Hatfield, Annie
Clark, Sam McKinniss, Cara
Yarmolowicz, Matthew
Sukiennik, Ian Bosak, Olivia
Jones, Brooke Kauffman, Katie
Coble, Ted Passon, Thomas
Lauria, Alix Lund, Matt Glassett,
Emily Cavanagh, Bill Schmidt,
and Dylan the Cat.

ISBN 978-1-942607-90-8